P9-DDN-434

Fake It Till You Break It

Fake It
TILL
YOU
Break It

JENN P. NGUYEN

SQUARE FISH

Swoon READS

NEW YORK

SQUARE
FISH

An imprint of Macmillan Publishing Group, LLC
120 Broadway, New York, NY 10271
fiercereads.com

FAKE IT TILL YOU BREAK IT. Copyright © 2019 by Jenn P. Nguyen.
All rights reserved. Printed in the United States of America.

Square Fish and the Square Fish logo are trademarks of Macmillan and
are used by Swoon Reads under license from Macmillan.

Our books may be purchased in bulk for promotional, educational, or business use.
Please contact your local bookseller or the Macmillan Corporate and Premium Sales
Department at (800) 221-7945 ext. 5442 or by email at MacmillanSpecialMarkets@
macmillan.com.

Library of Congress Control Number: 2018955579
ISBN 978-1-250-25084-1 (paperback)   ISBN 978-1-250-30802-3 (ebook)

Originally published in the United States by Swoon Reads
First Square Fish edition, 2020
Book designed by Carol Ly
Square Fish logo designed by Filomena Tuosto

10 9 8 7 6 5 4 3 2 1

To my dad, my number one biggest fan.
I miss you every single day.
Con thương bố' nhi`êu lắm.

MIA

IF THERE'S ONE THING I'm grateful for in my life, it's that arranged marriages aren't common anymore. At least not in Hempstead, Texas.

I mean, yeah, I'm also glad that I'm alive and that my mom is happy and healthy and all that stuff. Oh, and my hair has finally stopped doing that frizzy thing in the morning that usually takes at least twenty minutes to straighten.

And for the absence of Meatloaf Mondays at school. Or rather Mystery Mondays because I'm not sure what they did to make the meat harden like a can of Play-Doh that had been left out in the sun for a week. One of life's biggest mysteries. Whatever it was, it finally got taken off the menu for good. Sometimes it sucks that I can't leave school grounds until I'm a senior next year.

But today, I was definitely most grateful about the whole

arranged-marriage thing. Especially as my mom tugged on my shirt for the tenth time while I tried to usher her out the door.

"Seriously, Mom, if we don't leave right this second, I'm going to miss first period, which will result in me failing calculus. Then I'll have to drop out of school and end up living here with you forever." Clasping my fingers around her wrist, I dragged her across the porch. Well, attempted to. It was like trying to move a boulder. Or me out of bed on a Sunday morning. "Just you, me, and a dozen dogs I'm going to adopt. Big, drooling, fluffy ones."

My threats did nothing to faze her. "We have time. Why are you wearing *this* shirt again?" Her fingers rubbed on my left sleeve as though she were trying to make the violet color fade. "I swear, Mia, I always buy you such pretty outfits, and you never wear any of them."

"You mean you always buy me pretty *blue* outfits. You know I hate the color blue."

"Nonsense. No one could hate the color blue. It's the color of the sky. Do you hate the sky?"

Rolling my eyes, I let go of her and crossed my arms. "Yes, I hate the sky. It's on the list of top five things I hate along with ice cream, freshly cut grass, and puppies. Especially cute round corgis that like to roll around and frolic in grassy green meadows. So. Annoying."

Her left eyebrow rose. "You shouldn't be so sarcastic this early in the morning. It's bad for your indigestion."

"It's okay. Walmart has a two-for-one sale for Tums this week. I'll pick them up along with some Red Bull and batteries to give you some energy."

Instead of responding, she just let out a heavy sigh as if the weight of the world's problems was on her shoulders. Or maybe it was. It certainly wasn't easy having me for a daughter. Something she told me weekly.

Basking in my triumph of getting the last word in, I reached out and grabbed the keys from her hand. "If you're not in the car in two minutes, I'm leaving without you."

She gaped at me, both hands on her hips. "Excuse me, who exactly is the parent around here?"

"Something I wonder all the time," I muttered under my breath.

To be honest, I didn't hate the sky. Or ice cream and corgis. You'd have to be some sort of psycho to hate corgis. Although freshly cut grass did stir up my allergies like crazy, so I wasn't exactly fond of that. But I especially didn't hate the color blue. In fact, I loved it, but I could never wear it. The problem was the *reason* my mom insisted on me wearing blue *all the time*— from scrunchies and earrings to socks and underwear. And that was because blue was *Jake's* favorite color.

Damn Jake Adler. Number one on my hate list. He's the real reason I would rather wear a dress of fresh grass than wear blue. Ever.

Speaking of Mr. Number One . . .

Across the street, Mrs. Adler dragged him toward us with a determined look on her face. Suddenly Mom's reluctance to leave made sense. I quickened my pace.

The pain of having to go to school was only shadowed when our moms made us go *together*. Always together. No matter what. Family vacations, Sunday brunches, heck, even dentist appointments with Jake weren't enough. No, they schemed for us to go to school together every chance they got.

Last week, we avoided this by waking up at different times, but Jake's mom and my mom caught on pretty quickly. Now they were our own personal alarm clocks. And sometimes Mom's way of waking me up included cold water that she flicked on my face until I woke up. Harsh but effective. I'm glad she didn't just dump it on me. Probably didn't want the extra laundry.

Jake's feet shuffled against the asphalt so hard that I expected the rubber to be scraped off his navy sneakers by the time he reached our house.

As soon as Mom spotted them, she let out a little squeal that she immediately tried to cover up with a cough. "Oh my God, I completely forgot that I had plans with Jake's mom today. I don't think I could drive you to school after all."

I gave her a blank stare and leaned against the hood of my car. "Gee, isn't that funny how things worked out? And on the day that your car is in the shop."

"It's not *my* fault that my car needed to have the brakes

replaced." Her hand fluttered dramatically against her chest as she gasped. "You think I *wanted* my brakes to be faulty and be recalled at the factory? We're just lucky we didn't get into an accident beforehand. You could be at my *funeral* right now."

It's easy to see where I got my flair for theatrics. And I wasn't buying any of it. Still, I surrendered my car keys to her. "Yeah . . . and when did you say you were going to get your car back again?"

She brushed a strand of hair off of her face. Slowly. Delicately. "Oh, it may take all day. They're probably going to check the car for other stuff. Just in case. It's better to be thorough."

"If you need a ride, Mia, Jake would be happy to drive you," Mrs. Adler announced as she strolled up our sidewalk with Jake in tow. Both his hands were shoved into his jeans pockets. His dark hair was still damp and curled slightly around the nape of his neck and forehead. She must have dragged him out of the shower or something to get over here so quickly. "And he could drive you home, too."

Jake sighed. "Happy isn't exactly the word I would choose."

"Plus, if that was the case, I'd rather walk," I muttered under my breath.

But Mom's superhuman ears heard me. "If that's what you want. You could use the exercise after lying around the house all weekend."

Ouch. That was low. Especially because I'm pretty sure my extra baby fat and slightly round cheeks came from her side of the family. Everyone always said we were spitting images of each other. Something that delighted her to no end.

"By the way, Mia, you look soo pretty today." Mrs. Adler elbowed Jake's side. Her other hand played with the strap of the large tan tote bag slung over her shoulder. The metal tassels of the SeaWorld key chain from our Orlando trip four years ago swung back and forth. "Doesn't she look pretty?"

He shrugged, and she elbowed him even harder until he grimaced. "She looks the same as usual."

Mom clasped her hands together. "That's soo sweet of you." She stressed the soo the same way Mrs. Adler did, like it was a two-syllable word. "Wasn't that a nice compliment, Mia?"

"I don't know if that counts as a com—ouch!" Now it was Mom's turn to shove her elbow into my side. "I mean, yeah, thanks."

I met Jake's gaze, and we both rolled our eyes in unison. Could they *be* more obvious?

I'm not sure when or who came up with the crazy idea that Jake and I were destined to be together in the first place. Although I'll bet my savings that it was Mom's idea. Ever since she became a wedding planner, she had romance etched in her brain.

Whoever it was, this was something that Mom and Mrs. Adler had pursued with a passion since we were two.

Scorching, melt-your-ice-cream-in-two-seconds type of passion. Despite the fact that Jake and I could barely stand being in the same room together now. But our disdain for each other was just a minor blip in their dreams of being future in-laws. After all, according to Mom, someone had to take one for the team.

Still rubbing my aching waist, I straightened up. "Let's just go. I still have to meet with my chem group before homeroom."

With a bright smile, Mrs. Adler wrapped an arm around Mom's shoulders. "Of course. You don't want to be late. Jake, honey, you should carry Mia's bag out to the car for her."

"Huh?"

"Her. Bag."

"She has arms. Why should I—ouch! Mom!" With one hand rubbing his knee, Jake half walked, half wobbled away from her outstretched leg. The toe of her left black pump was still pointed at him. "I'll hold that for you."

I kept a tight grip on the strap and yanked back. "No, I'm fine."

"Just hand it over, will you?" he muttered under his breath. "Before I have to waste my health insurance on a broken leg."

Reluctantly, I surrendered my bag and walked toward his car across the street. "Fine. Whatever."

Jake and I didn't say anything else to each other until we were safely in his car and out of earshot of our moms. He turned on the ignition and grasped the side of my headrest as he slowly pulled out of the driveway. "Is it just me, or are they soo annoying?"

Snorting, I slouched down in the seat and pulled my knees up to prop them against the leather dashboard. No need to adjust the seat because it was already set perfectly to my almost five-foot, three-inch height. I've been in this seat more than I've been in my own car. The cushions were probably molded to my butt by now, flat as it was. "Well, subtlety was never their strong point. That's probably why they're such good friends."

"Right. That and their love for green tea lattes." Jake turned on the radio, and our moment of peaceful truce ended.

Seriously, sometimes I think Mom needed a new hobby. Knitting. Gardening. Collecting rare minted coins. Anything was better than throwing her only daughter into an arranged relationship with an annoying Know-It-All Ass.

He glanced over at me like he knew I was thinking about him. "By the way, you have purple jam on your left cheek."

It was probably raspberry jam left over from breakfast. I had toast and peanut butter with jam. Peach jam would have been better, but we were out.

"I'm leaving it to snack on during second period," I said blankly without moving.

Grimacing, he turned away. His hand rubbed the back of his neck until it turned pink.

It took everything I had not to laugh—although my lips couldn't help quirking up into a grin. I had to turn my face toward the window so he wouldn't notice and realize I was screwing with him on purpose.

His crazy obsession with being neat was something I had loved to mess with him about since we were eight. I couldn't help it. Jake was such a weird kid. He'd line up all his toy trucks according to size and color and not let anyone touch them. So, of course, I deliberately mixed them up, annoying the hell out of him. Finally, he ended up hiding all his cars in his room and locking his door.

That was also the year that our nicknames for each other—Ass and Brat—were born. Although my name for him always got me grounded whenever anyone heard me.

Such an unjust world we live in.

Jake rolled down the window an inch or two, and the wind ruffled his dark hair. The curls were cut close to the top of his ears. His fingertips drummed an erratic beat on the peeling steering wheel. "What time will you be done later?"

I crossed my arms. "You seriously don't need to pick me up. I'll just catch a ride home with someone else."

"It's fine. I need to watch the store for a few hours while Mr. MacArthur goes to his dentist appointment anyway, so I can stop by afterward. Besides I can't go home without you. Not in one piece anyway."

"Fine, do whatever you want."

He snorted. "Yeah, I'm pretty sure what I want doesn't matter. It never does." Before I could respond, he pulled into our school's parking lot. "So, what? Six? Seven?"

Snatching my bag from the back seat, I jumped out of the car. "Make it seven thirty."

"Damn, that's late." Letting out a long-suffering sigh, Jake climbed out of the car and came over to my side. Without saying anything else, he leaned over until he was right in my face.

Surprised, I backed up a bit, but he just took another step forward until he reached out . . . to brush against the corner of my mouth. Before I could say or do anything, he wiped the little smear of jam onto my sleeve.

"God, that had been annoying me the whole car ride," he said, shaking his head.

The hell . . . ?

I jerked away from him. "You're crazy, you know that?"

"Yeah, well, what do you expect when I'm forced to put up with you my entire life? I'm lucky you didn't put me in an insane asylum by now." He waved at Aly, who was waiting on our bench by the parking lot, before walking away. "See you at seven thirty."

I was still sputtering when Aly came up to me. "What was that about?"

My fingers rubbed at the corner of my mouth, and I scowled. "Nothing. Just Jake being an ass as usual."

MIA

MY EYES GAZED LONGINGLY at the stage. Lyndon Whitmore, the lead actress, sang about her family's journey across the river as she danced across the stage, light as a gazelle. Her voice rang out loud and clear across the partially empty auditorium. I made a note of her posture and how she lifted her head. I even attempted to purse my lips the same way she did, but I knew I could never sound the same. Not unless I could steal her voice like in *The Little Mermaid*.

Talented people sure are easy to hate sometimes.

I mean, I wasn't horrible—despite the fact that Jake said roosters crowing sounded better than my singing.

When I was seven, I took voice lessons that cost Mom way too much money, but all they did was make me enunciate my words more. Something I probably could have learned from *Sesame Street*.

But, *how* did Lyndon do that? It seemed so effortless for

her. Like drinking water. Or riding a bike. Although that was a pretty bad example because I never actually learned how to ride a bike. Apparently, I had no sense of balance along with being tone-deaf. Jake tried to teach me when we were ten, but he got so frustrated that he ended up just paying me to give up.

Easiest fifty bucks I ever made.

Someone tapped the back of my head, knocking me out of my daydream. Aly plopped down on the seat beside me. "Your eyes are going to fall out if you keep glaring at Lyndon like that."

"I wasn't glaring. I was . . . examining her technique."

"Uh-huh. And does your examination include scowling, too?" Without waiting for my answer, she handed over her cup of coffee—extra cream and two sugars.

Holding the cup up to my nose, I breathed in the lovely aroma a few times before letting out a happy sigh. I didn't actually like the taste of coffee, but the smell was enough to perk me up. "Thanks, I needed that. It's been a really long day. But any day I'm forced to see Jake is a long day."

Aly snorted. "That's every day then. Maybe we should all carpool sometime. Save gas and the environment and all that. Or you could take my car, and I'll carpool with him."

"Urgh, why would you do that?"

She swept her honey-brown locks into a low ponytail. "Uh, 'cause he's cute?"

Wait, what? My left eyebrow rose, and I reached out to touch her forehead. Cool as a cucumber. So, she's not delirious from being sick. "Are you *crazy*?"

She batted my hand away. "Are you *blind*? He's adorable. Like, hot boy next door who doesn't even realize that he's hot. Which makes him even hotter. And he's so nice, too. Well, maybe not to *you*, but he's nice to me. And to everyone else. He's Mr. Good Guy."

Gagging, I handed back her cup of coffee. "Take this before I puke in it and make you waste three bucks."

"Four. I added an extra shot of espresso and soy milk. And come on. I know you hate the guy, but even you have to admit that he's pretty easy on the eyes."

Easy on the eyes?

I scratched my head, but I just couldn't see what she was talking about. I mean, yeah, I guess his hazel eyes were nice. Especially since he finally got rid of those Coke-bottle glasses and wore contacts. Without them, he was practically blind. When we were kids, all I had to do to win at hide-and-seek with him was steal his glasses. Sixty-seven wins. Once just by sitting on the couch with a matching blanket.

And he was . . . tall?

"Hot and adorable aren't exactly words I'd ever use to describe Jake. Those words are reserved for someone like . . . like . . ."

"Ben Grayson?" Even though Aly meant to whisper, her

naturally loud voice echoed across the auditorium. And just our luck, this was also when everyone onstage was taking a break so it was deadly silent.

Ben was sitting at the corner of the stage talking to Daniel, the theater director, but he jumped to his feet when he heard his name. I had to wave both hands away 'cause God knows I didn't know what I would say to him if he did come over.

Confused, he sat back down, but not before giving me an endearing half smile that made my knees weak like they were made of floppy lime Jell-O. Good thing I was sitting on a chair or I'm pretty sure I would have face-planted right on the floor.

My cheeks exploded, but I grinned back as I stapled the second act scene's script together for the next rehearsal. Thankfully, my hands automatically moved through the routine motions because I couldn't really concentrate on anything else.

I knew I was acting like a complete idiot, but this was BEN GRAYSON. I didn't know his middle name, but it was probably "Perfect." My crush bloomed the moment my eyes met his clear chocolate eyes across the auditorium, and it had only grown in the past few months.

Ben was a senior. In fact, the *only* senior to receive an early admission to UC San Diego. He could have ditched this town to start college in August. But to everyone's surprise, he turned them down. Instead he chose to ride out the rest of his senior year by being the understudy for Leon MacDonald, the main lead in the musical.

To be honest, he could have easily been the lead, but he wanted to learn all parts of the theater. Including being an understudy. But that was who Ben was. Dedicated. And funny. Handsome. Almost on the verge of a pretty boy, but a little more boyish. Mischievous. Like he was thinking of a joke but would never tell you the punch line.

Sigh. Basically the man of my dreams.

Aly snapped her fingers in front of my face to get my attention. "If you could stop drooling over Ben for a minute, your idol is about to pass. If you want to talk to Lyndon, now's your chance."

Straightening in my seat, I let out a slow deep breath like Mom's yoga instructors taught us. In and out. In and out. "Hey, Lyndon?"

She stopped a few feet away and cocked her head in our direction. Her fingers twisted around the strap of her bag on her skinny shoulder. "Yeah?"

"I was wondering . . . if you think you could . . . if you're free . . ." My sentences kept fading off the longer she stood there in front of us. "If you—you wanted to take a look at the script for tomorrow's rehearsal."

Lyndon patted her bag. "Daniel already gave it to me."

"Oh, okay then. I guess I'll see you tomorrow."

"See you."

Aly waited until she left before letting out a low whistle. "What the heck was *that*? I thought you were going to ask her for pointers and stuff?"

I banged my forehead against the top of the table. "I wanted to. But I just . . . couldn't."

"But why?"

Because the longer Lyndon stood there—the more I stared at her—the more it became apparent how different we were. And that I could never be like her. Even the attempt would be too much for me.

Two years ago, I volunteered to usher for a show on a whim to get out of yet another family dinner with the Adlers. But as soon as the curtains opened and the show started, I fell in love. To this day, I don't even remember what the show was about. But it didn't matter. Nothing else did except for the emotions that swept over me as I sat there. Even long after everyone else left and the ushers were sweeping the trash from the aisles. The amazement of the actors' confidence onstage. The thrill of everyone watching, enwrapped in their every word. Every movement. Although I'd never been here before, it felt exactly like home.

This was where I belonged. This was *my* place. And my dream was to be onstage one day. Although if I were dreaming, then might as well wish to be on Broadway, but to be honest, I'd be satisfied with any stage at this point.

Sometimes a tiny part of me—the ugly, realist, annoying part that I named Cecily after my fourth-grade torturer, I mean, teacher—kept mocking me. That I needed to stop kidding myself. I wasn't good enough to perform. Probably never would be. And doing theater grunt work was probably going to be the highlight of my sad, pathetic life. And I should be satisfied with just watching the show or putting stamps on flyers.

Thankfully, Ol' Cece would only butt in every once in a while. But she would get louder and louder every time. And she was becoming much harder to ignore. Especially as senior year and graduation came closer and closer. To the real world where I'd have to face reality and give up this dream. And realize that some things were just out of my reach.

But I couldn't explain all of this to Aly. All I could do was bang my head harder on the table.

JAKE

INSTEAD OF ORDERING, the guy stood in front of the toppings station and pointed a stubby finger at me. His eyes narrowed as he leaned forward. "You look familiar. Are you on YouTube or something?"

"No, not at all." I ducked my head down so the guy couldn't look that closely at my face.

"Are you sure? 'Cause you really look like one of those dudes—"

Jeez, just order already. "Definitely sure. Now, how would you like this dressed?" My hand automatically reached for the lettuce because that was what people usually wanted on their sandwiches.

"Hmm." He stared at me for another minute or two before shrugging. "Just mayo. And make sure it's the fat-free kind. Do you know if it's gluten-free?"

Freezing, I eyed the guy in front of me a little more closely. The huge sumo-wrestler-looking dude in front of me. His brown hair was slicked back off of his forehead with a navy headband. And his shirt looked like it was a size or two too small. Maybe I heard him wrong. "Uh, sorry, I just know that it's low fat. So just the mayo?"

"Yeah, and make it a thin line." He held up his beefy thumb and index finger that were pressed together like I didn't know what the word *thin* meant.

". . . okay." I grabbed the mayo bottle and squeezed.

"Thinner."

My hand slowed, and I released the pressure on the bottle.

Thin Mayo Dude scowled. "No, less—shit, don't you know how to make a decent sandwich?"

Decent sandwich? This was barely worth standing in line for. And definitely not worth $8.95. God damn it, I hated working here sometimes. Correction. Most of the time.

Whatever. It's his money he's wasting.

Suppressing my sigh, I forced a smile on my face instead. "Sorry." This time I spread a line so thin that you couldn't even see the mayo.

"Finally." He looked at the watch on his wrist. "And can you make it quick? I have to go. Just a Coke with very few ice cubes."

"Sure thing, she'll ring you up." I wrapped up the sad excuse for a sandwich and thankfully passed it along to Rose. He was her problem now. I wouldn't be surprised if the dude wanted to count the ice cubes in his drink.

She smiled brightly at him before turning to get his drink. Instantly, the dude's grumpy frown made a complete 180 as he watched her. There were practically hearts shooting out of his eyes. Rose had that effect on a lot of people. Too bad they didn't know that she was most likely thinking snarky thoughts about everyone. Her angelic face was the perfect cover-up. The only person who got to see her real side was her brother, Greg, and me. Benefits of being her best friend, I guess.

When Thin Mayo Dude finally left, Rose reached around me and pulled the piping hot trays of cookies out of the oven to cool. We were instantly surrounded with sweet sugary smells of chocolate and oatmeal. She popped in the new trays of wheat bread and set the timer.

Practically drooling since I hadn't eaten dinner yet, I grabbed a double chocolate cookie for myself. It burned my hand a bit but was totally worth it as my teeth sank into the soft chocolate. The free fresh cookies made the low pay and irritating customers sting a little less.

Rose propped herself up to sit on the metal counter. The tip of her left green sneaker kicked at the wooden stool between us. "So I got the tickets and backstage passes for the Lakeshore music festival next month for Greg and me. And it's still not too late to sign up. I could talk to the coordinator on your behalf. It's all new up-and-coming artists, so I'm sure we could get you a spot. We could even carpool."

This was the fourth time she had brought up the festival this week. I swallowed the scalding hot cookie and shook my head. "Nah, Mom's landscaping the backyard, and I promised I'd help her out. You know, with the rocks and trees and heavy-lifting stuff."

Rose nodded and pulled out her phone. "Fine, I'll let Greg convince you."

I groaned. "Seriously? I thought we were friends."

"We are. Best friends. I love you even more than my own brother. And that's why I'm doing this for your own good." She typed something on the screen before slipping the phone back into her pocket with a grin. "Done."

Immediately, my phone started buzzing with messages. I didn't need to look at the screen to know that it was probably being flooded with texts from Greg. He was like a hound dog. Never let anything go. And Rose knew it.

Just like she knew me. Helping Mom was a lame excuse. Hell, I was kind of embarrassed that I couldn't think of something better.

I tossed my napkin at her and grabbed another cookie. "I'm going to cut some more veggies. We're low on tomatoes. Watch the front for a bit."

Rounding the corner, I went into the cooler in the back of

the store. But instead of grabbing the box of tomatoes on the bottom shelf, I leaned back against the cold metal wall and sighed.

To be honest, the festival sounded like it could be fun. Rose had been planning on doing a webcast on the festival for ages. She made a bunch of them to bulk up her resume. Her dream was to travel and let everyone experience the world through her videos. Greg, on the other hand, probably just wanted to go to hook up with girls. Both plans sounded pretty awesome, though.

Either way, it would be a blast to hang out with them. Chill and relax. Listen to some new musicians and take advantage of the weather before it got too hot. In another time, that would have exactly been my scene. Before Finn left. Now I had sworn off all of that.

My phone went off again. But a different ringtone this time. Reserved to warn me of calls and texts from Finn.

Even if it weren't for the ringtone, I'd still know it was him. Finn always texted me around this time from the cruise ship. Like clockwork. It didn't matter if I never responded. Which I never did. Why should I? He was the one who left us right after graduation years ago. And barely a glance back or a wave goodbye to Mom and me. No phone calls. No emails. Nothing for practically two years.

And now, out of the blue, he suddenly wants to talk to us again? Mom talked to him every time, but I didn't. Why should I? He had a family, and he ditched us. Simple as that. Just because he suddenly remembered *now* that he had a brother didn't mean I had to accept it.

I crammed the last of the chocolate cookie in my mouth and dusted my hands on my black apron. Whatever. Time to get back to work before I picked up Mia. Those tomatoes weren't going to cut themselves.

TWO HOURS LATER, I almost ran a red light racing to the theater. Crap, I was late. REALLY late.

There was a cherry soda explosion just as Mr. MacArthur came back, so by the time I actually left the store, it was already almost eight. The theater's parking lot was nearly empty by then, but I could see Mia pacing around Carly's car. Carly was this older chick who was the assistant director for the play Mia was helping out in. Something about . . . families? I think. She told me what it was about, but to be honest, I didn't really remember. Mia talked a lot.

Judging by the way Mia was stomping her feet, I could tell she was pissed. I could practically see waves of irritation radiating off her body.

Great. First I had to deal with Thin Mayo Dude, then the soda explosion, and now this. Plus, my shirt was damp and sticky with soda. And I was pretty sure some of it was still in my hair. I had rushed out to pick up Mia and didn't get to clean up. I could still feel it on my scalp. And it wasn't a good feeling.

I pulled up next to the silver Accord. "Sorry I'm late. Let's go home."

Mia crossed her scrawny arms and didn't budge. "You said you were only going to be a *little* late. If I had known it would take this long, I would have taken the bus or something."

"Yeah, well, I could have been a lot later, so just be thankful for that. Now, can you move your ass?"

Still grumbling, she finally pulled open the car door and hopped in. "I swear I'm too nice. I should have just let you go home and deal with your mom on your own. Don't know why I even bothered."

I rolled my eyes at her martyr act. "Uh, you bothered because you knew that *your* mom would have been on your back all night if you didn't come home with me."

She wrinkled her nose but didn't deny it.

Satisfied that I got the last word for once, I leaned over Mia's lap and waved at Carly. "Thanks for keeping her company."

She crossed her arms and smirked at us like we were a couple of kids she was babysitting. "No problem. Anything for Mia's boyfriend."

Mia shoved at my shoulder in front of her, but I deliberately didn't move to piss her off. If anything, I leaned into her even more, practically lying on top of her. At least until she elbowed me in the ribs. Hard. With a grunt, I sat back in my seat.

"You know we're not dating. I have better taste than that," Mia complained as she pulled the rearview mirror down and combed her dark hair with her fingertips.

Carly just laughed as she walked back to her car. Her black boots clicked against the pavement. "Sure, you're not. Not now anyway."

"Not ever," I called out as we pulled away. We sat in silence for a few minutes while Mia continued to fix her hair. "So she's nice. A little crazy, but nice."

She rolled her eyes and finally sat back. Her pink lips pursed together. "I think you mean a lot crazy. I mean, come on, us together?"

"True. That would be like if owls and hawks mated."

"Exactly. Although I'm assuming that you're the owl since you're a nerd."

I snorted. "Says the girl with a Harry Potter phone case."

"Hey, you were the one who got it for me!"

"Only because my mom made me." I switched on the left turn signal and merged into the lane. "Hold on, I need to grab some coffee to study tonight. Want anything?"

"Like I said, nerd." Her fingertips tapped against the car door in a steady rhythm as I pulled into the drive-through line. "And no, I'm good."

Sure she was.

There was static on the other end of the intercom. "Hi. Can I . . . your order?"

"Can you hold on for a minute?" I chewed on my thumbnail and studied the menu. What did I want? Something sweet, but I needed some major caffeine. There was a world-history report due in a few days and I barely had a topic and I was exhausted today. It was going to be a long night.

Mia undid her seat belt and leaned over me. Her left hand braced against my arm as she balanced herself over my lap. Her dark hair practically touched my crotch. Our faces were barely inches apart. I could count her lashes if I wanted to. I should shove her away like she did to me, but I didn't move. "Yeah, could I have a grande caffe mocha with an extra shot of espresso? And two blueberry scones? Thanks."

". . .'kay. Come to the . . ."

The hell? My brow rose as I pulled up to the next window. "What was that?"

Mia widened her eyes and tried to look innocent. And failed miserably. "Come on, you were taking forever like you always do. And you know you were going to order that anyway."

I wanted to argue with her, but her order did sound like it would hit the spot. Right down to the two blueberry scones. And as much as I hated to admit it, she was right. Didn't mean she needed to know that. She was already annoying enough as it is. I don't know how she knew what I wanted before I did, though.

With a sigh, I absentmindedly rubbed my arm where she had held it before. For some reason, it was all hot and felt weird. In fact, the whole car was really hot all of a sudden. I cranked up the air conditioner to full blast and adjusted both sides to point at me.

Mia continued chatting like she didn't feel the temp change. "I don't know why you always order two of everything. You never finish it."

My mouth twisted into a wry half grin. "Maybe I like wasting money."

"You're so weird."

Snorting to myself, I just shook my head. Funny how she noticed that I always ordered two of everything, but not the reason why. 'Cause the truth was if I didn't, I'd never get to eat anything at all. Fifteen years' experience taught me how to survive with Mia around.

Within ten minutes, I was proved right as half of a blueberry scone was gone. Mia kept bobbing her head to the song on the radio as she picked at the scone with her left hand. I had no idea how she ate without thinking all the time.

There were a couple of crumbs around the left corner of her mouth. I would have told her, but I didn't want her to realize she was eating the scone. Or worse, that I always bought an extra one for her. She might think I actually cared about her or something. Then I'd never hear the end of it.

Instead, I took a deep sip of my drink. Just the right amount of bitterness to cut through the sweet frothy drink. Kind of like Mia herself.

Sometimes she wasn't so bad. If it weren't for our moms shoving us together all the time, we might even be friends.

Maybe.

JAKE

MY FINGERS TAPPED an erratic rhythm against my laptop cover, and I let out a heavy sigh. "For the last time, Greg, I'm not going. And if you ask me again, I'm going to block your number from my phone."

He snorted on the other end of the line. "Okay, okay, don't get your panties in a bunch. I was just making sure because if you change your mind, there won't be any openings left. You know, maybe you need to think about it overnight and get back to me—"

"That's it, I'm hanging up on you."

"Come on, Jake, just—"

Click.

I shut off my phone in case he called again. If he weren't Rose's brother, I would have decked him through the phone. Although I'm sure she wouldn't have minded.

Rose and I became friends in elementary school. We were

both in the same honors class and usually partnered together. I guess it had been only a matter of time until I'd meet Greg, since they were twins after all.

But he wasn't all bad. As crazy as he was, Greg was like a brother to me, too. An annoying, irritating little brother whom no one would buy no matter how much you tried to sell him for. No wonder he got along awesome with Mia.

Luckily, nobody knew that the coordinator had already contacted me. Apparently, she stumbled on our YouTube channel a few weeks ago. She seemed super disappointed that the Adler Brothers no longer existed, but she was still keen to have me perform. I haven't given her an answer yet. I should. But then I should do a lot of things.

Like now.

My mouse hovered over the delete button on our YouTube account to get rid of it once and for all. I'd been meaning to do it for ages, but my finger never seemed to want to pull the trigger. Or rather click the button. Today was no exception. I half hoped that if I avoided the site long enough, the account would delete itself.

This was stupid. *I* was stupid. Keeping a couple of videos we made when we were kids wasn't going to bring Finn back. Not that I even wanted him to come back. It wasn't going to change anything.

Just then Mom poked her head in. "Could I come in?"

I slammed the laptop shut and twisted around in my chair. "Sure."

She settled onto the edge of my bed and crossed her ankles. "So, Greg called the house a couple of times. Said your cell phone was turned off or something?"

"Oh, you don't need to worry about him."

"Who said I was worried?" Mom smiled and leaned back against the mattress on her hands. It squeaked a bit at her movement. "I figured you must be avoiding his calls for a good reason, so I told him you were showering. Pretty sure he didn't believe me, but he was too scared to argue."

"You're the best. I'll deal with him on Monday."

"Good luck with that. So, want to tell me what that's all about?"

Shaking my head, I kicked at a book on the carpet. "Just some dumb music festival he wants me to go to with him and Rose. Probably just to drive because he's a lazy ass."

"Takes one to know one," Mom joked. "So, do you have your suit ready for tomorrow?"

"Tomorrow . . . ?"

"The wedding?" At the continued blank look on my face, she let out a sigh and crossed her arms. "Don't tell me that you forgot."

"No, I didn't forget. I just didn't remember." I scratched my head. "Whose wedding is this again?"

"It's Mrs. Le's second cousin on her mom's side." She stopped and bit the tip of her thumb. "Or is it her first cousin?"

"Now look who doesn't remember." I tried not to sound too smug, but it didn't work.

It wasn't Mom's fault, though. Mia was related to practically the entire town. Everyone was a cousin or aunt or something. My tiny family seemed sad and lonely. Mom loved the Les' giant family, though. The noise and chaos. Sometimes I wondered why she and Uncle Bran never had kids of their own. Although that was probably a blessing in disguise, since he disappeared soon after Mom—at the time, Aunt Lily—took us in after our real parents died.

"So, if you don't even know who's getting married, then why are we invited?"

"Well, technically, we're not. We're . . . going as Mrs. Le's and Mia's plus ones."

Ah, and there it was.

I didn't even bother to fight her about it. Since Mom loved these weddings so much, I tried not to put up *too* much of a fuss whenever Mom wrangled me into going with her. Even though I knew that it was partly a ploy to get me to hang out with Mia more.

Plus, the cake was always pretty good. The seven-course meal never hurt, either.

Still looking guilty, Mom cleared her throat. "What were

you looking at before closing your laptop? College applications? Porn?"

I grimaced and pretended to gag. Well, half pretended. Just hearing Mom say the word *porn* was enough to send chills down my spine. "Please don't ever say that to me again. Ever."

Her eyes widened with fake innocence. "Jeez, I didn't know you were so sensitive about college applications."

"Ha ha, very funny."

"I try." She tapped against my green bedsheets, scratching at the surface a bit with her nails. "But seriously, have you looked at college stuff yet? I know you still have over a year to think about it, but I'd kind of like a heads-up. Like whether I should be renting out your room or something."

I snorted. "Like you would let a stranger in here. Hell, Finn's room is still a shrine, and it's bigger than mine."

Mom's face fell a bit. "That's true."

The room got quiet, and I was instantly sorry I brought him up. He was a sore point between us. Hell, he was a sore point, period.

After our parents died nearly fifteen years ago, Mom was the one who brought us home. Who kept us together and quit her job as marketing director at a tutoring center just so she could stay at home with us. To take us to school and daycare, nurse us when we were sick, make peanut butter and jelly sandwiches (crustless for Finn), and come to all of our soccer practices. She even went back to her maiden name, Adler, so we wouldn't feel left out. And although she swears it wasn't our fault, I know we were the real reason Uncle Bran left.

It didn't take a genius to figure that out. They were a blissfully happy married couple one minute and then we moved in and they weren't. He didn't want to be saddled with two kids who weren't even his. Mia and I overheard her and Mrs. Le talking about it a few weeks after he left.

That was also the first time I ever saw Mom cry.

And yet, after everything she did—everything she gave up—how did Finn repay her? By ditching town to work at some cruise line the instant he graduated. That was the second time she ever cried.

Ungrateful ass.

I forced a smile onto my face for her benefit. "I haven't really thought about college yet, but I'll probably go to Houston for college, Mom. It's not too far. I mean, I don't even know what I'm majoring in yet. Going out of state would just be a waste of money."

Mom let out a sigh of relief that she tried to cover up with a laugh. She brushed her bangs out of her eyes. "Oh, okay. I mean, I don't want you to think I'm forcing you to stay here with me. You're free to do whatever you want. Spread your wings and leave the nest. All that poetic stuff."

"I don't need all that poetic stuff." I stacked my hands behind my neck. "I'm fine right here."

Her smile turned suspiciously sweet. "Right here with Mia?"

I rolled my eyes. "We're not having this conversation again."

"I swear, there's so much chemistry radiating between you two every time you're together, I practically need sunglasses. If only you could just TRY dating her. Just once. For me?"

"Mom, that's hatred between us. Not chemistry." With a snort, I leaned back against my chair. It squeaked every time I pushed backward. "Seriously, we haven't gotten along since we were kids. I don't think playing house when you're five means Cupid's going to come running with his bow."

She pursed her lips for a few seconds before letting out a long sigh. "Fine, I can see that you're not ready to accept the truth yet. I'm willing to wait a bit longer."

"Like forever?"

I was surprised that she was giving up so soon. Usually she could ramble on and on about Mia until morning. About how sweet she was. How the sunlight glinted off her shiny dark hair and lit up her eyes. How contagious her laugh was. If it were up to Mom, we'd be getting married after high school and alternate weeks living here and at the Les' house.

"Anyway, I wanted to talk to you about something else," Mom continued. "Mrs. Le and I have been talking about where to go for vacation this summer, and we decided that a cruise would be fun. Maybe to the Bahamas . . ."

A cruise? My eyes narrowed at the direction this conversation was going. Especially when she looked away, suddenly really interested in the books on my shelf. "And did you decide on which cruise line?"

"Actually, we did. The Emerald cruises sounded nice. Clean, delicious food, affordable, great on-board entertainment. It has three water slides and a rooftop miniature-golf course. It even has a huge arcade and bowling alley on the third floor!"

I crossed my arms. "Wait, let's go back to the on-board entertainment. How do you know that it's great?"

Finally, she looked over at me. Guilt etched across her entire face like a banner. "It's the cruise ship your brother works on."

Even though I suspected this was what she was getting at, it still hit me like a ton of bricks. How could she even think about seeing *him*? That she could make *me* see him? My vision got a bit blurry, and I blinked furiously to gape at her. "Are you serious? Why the hell would you want to go there? And see *him*?"

"Now, Jake, I know you're upset—"

I scoffed. "I'm not upset. That jackass doesn't deserve me caring enough about him to be upset."

Now it was her turn to scowl. "He's still your brother. Your *older* brother. I won't have you talking about him like that."

"Even if he deserves it," I muttered under my breath before shutting up for good when she shot me a fierce glare. My stomach still twisted uncomfortably at the thought of going on this trip.

I've always known that Mom would welcome Finn back with open arms the second he came back someday, but this was even worse than anything I imagined. He wasn't coming back to see us. *We* were going to *him*. Like we were begging him to come back to us. To be in our lives. Like we *needed* him.

My hands curled into tight fists against my side.

Mom lightly touched my arm. "I know this is pretty sudden to you, but I've been thinking about this for a while. It's time to let everything go and be a family again. Before it's too late. And we've been apart long enough."

"But we *are* a family. You and me. Isn't that enough?"

She gave me a sad smile but didn't answer. Instead, she just got up and headed toward the door. "I'll give you time to let things sink in before we talk about it again. Good night."

Frustrated, I shoved myself away from my desk so hard that my folder slid off and my English report flew everywhere. Even my Little League trophy toppled over and landed facedown in my trash can.

Instead of cleaning up, I gave my trash can a good kick and flopped onto the bed with an arm over my face.

Did she think we would just go on this cruise and suddenly become one big happy family again? She had to be crazy. I mean, I loved Mom and everything. And I would do almost anything for her. Anything except for this. Even I had a limit to what I was willing to do. And seeing Finn's stupid face wasn't one of those things.

She could give me all the time in the world, but I wasn't going to change my mind. Nothing was going to make me want to see Finn again no matter what she said. The dude left us. Left our family. End of story.

But shit, how the hell was I going to get out of this one?

MIA

IT WAS NEARLY SIX when we finally made it to the reception hall. Half an hour late. Mom couldn't find her wedge nude heels. And she tore the entire house apart to find them. Seriously, my room looked like a freaking category-five hurricane hit. Which is just a tad worse than what it usually looked like.

The reception hall was already packed by the time we got there. Luckily, Mrs. Adler and Jake came early to save us seats. And they weren't hard to find, because they were two of the few guests who weren't Asian.

The bride, Ngoc, and the groom's family were just starting to line up by the stage, so we snuck in to sit at our table in the far-left corner. I tried to grab the seat on the other side of Mrs. Adler, but Mom plopped herself down and prodded me toward the empty seat beside Jake.

With a sigh, I waved at the family with three kids sitting

across the table. The youngest daughter, who looked about three, waved chocolate-stained fingers back at me. Looked like someone got to the chocolate fountain early.

Moving the lazy Susan in his direction, Jake grabbed some red sticky rice from the plate with the chopsticks like a pro. Then again, he spent enough meals at my house to maneuver the two sticks like they were an extension of his own hand. He offered the plate to Mom and Mrs. Adler, but ignored me. Instead, he swirled it around until the plate was on the opposite end of the table.

What. A. Dick. Even though I was starving, I leaned back into my seat and watched the bridal party shimmy across the room as the DJ shouted out their names. Concentrated on anything but my rumbling stomach. Thank goodness the booming dance music drowned me out.

Or at least I thought it did.

With dark wide eyes, the little girl gasped and rubbed her chocolate fingers all over her cheeks. Jake snorted under his breath and moved the lazy Susan until the plate of sticky rice was right in front of me. Not wanting to admit that I was starving, it took every ounce of willpower I had to move it away. Instead, I searched my purse until I found a mint and popped it into my mouth. It tasted a tad bit stale, but now wasn't the time to be picky.

Luckily, the couple was just starting their first dance. I straightened up in my seat and turned my head to watch them.

No matter how many weddings I've been to—and believe me, there have been a LOT because I occasionally help Mom with her weddings in the summer—this was always my favorite part. The bride grinned so widely that my own cheeks would hurt just looking at her. And the groom couldn't help staring at her with such joy as he whispered something in her ear. Sometimes their dances would be choreographed and be stiff, or they would just hold each other and sway before twirling a few times. Maybe there would be a dip or two. Sometimes it would be kind of cheesy. But it didn't matter. It was always beautiful.

According to Google, the average length of a marriage is eight years, and more than half ended in divorce. Tons of brides come back to my mom to plan their second or even third wedding.

But still . . . in that exact moment of every couple's first dance, all those numbers and facts didn't matter. Nothing did. This moment was so sweet that even the most cynical person couldn't help melting as they watched. Even if the statistics turned into 100 percent divorce, you just believed that *they* would be the ones who would make it.

As if on cue, my eyes started to well up. I fumbled for the napkin on the table before anyone else noticed. Just then, a pack of tissues landed on my lap.

I glanced over, but Jake just straightened his jacket and continued eating without looking over at me. I dabbed my eyes with a tissue, careful not to smear my makeup and lashes that took nearly forty-five minutes to apply. I had nearly poked my eyes out with the mascara wand, too. Not sure how those YouTube people could do it in five minutes.

After all the dances were done, the food finally came out. I almost cheered out loud at the sight of the crab and asparagus soup. Then swooned at the cute waiter who brought the bowl. Who only made things more awesome.

As we ate, Mom and Mrs. Adler pointed at us and giggled behind their hands, not very subtly. These weddings spurred them on the Jakia ship—their words, not mine—even more than usual. I mean, usually they were already pretty bad, but at weddings, they were crazy.

Jake and I did our best to ignore them and each other. It wasn't hard. Jake didn't say anything most of the night. All he did was scowl like a grumpy old man every time the DJ played a new song. So I concentrated on everyone else around us. There was a drunk uncle who kept coming up and dedicating songs to the couple, but he wasn't too bad. I've heard worse.

Our hottie waiter, Dan, would stop by our table every ten minutes to see how we were doing. And each time he did, I'd inch a little closer to him. He'd bend down a little farther to "hear" me. I could tell by his flirtatious grin that he was interested. Plus, he brought me a new Coke every time I ran out.

Now I just needed to somehow slip him my number without Mom seeing. It's been ages since I had a decent date. Not after the last time, when Mom ran Jimmy Sutton off. Seriously, you would have thought she was interrogating someone in a courtroom for murder. 'Course she did that to every guy who came by to see me whose name wasn't Jake. News of my crazy mom spread through the school like wildfire. Only a few guys dared to suffer her wrath.

Dylan Saunders. The freckly part-time server who occasionally worked the weddings Mom did.

Kirk Tran. The cute senior band captain with the amazingly craterlike dimples.

And Mike Le (no relation). The guy who accidentally got my smoothie order because the barista mixed up our orders.

The only thing these three guys had in common were our brief summer romances. All less than three weeks. It took me longer to watch the entire series of *Game of Thrones*. But Mom was busier in the summertime, so it was easier to date these guys behind her back. For a short time at least.

And my last date was Dylan in July. Nearly ten months ago. But hopefully my luck was about to change tonight. That is, if I could somehow sneak Dan my phone number before the night was over.

Desperate times called for desperate measures. I jumped up from my seat. "I'm going to get some dessert before they run out."

"Do you need Jake to go with you?" Mrs. Adler asked, poking Jake's arm.

"No!" I let out a short laugh and flexed. "I've been working out so I'm pretty sure I can hold a plate of cupcakes by myself. Be right back."

My heels clacked against the tile floor as I quickly ran away before my mom or Mrs. Adler could say anything else. I had seen Dan disappear toward the kitchen about five minutes ago, so I probably only had a minute or two before he came back out. A minute or two to position myself exactly by the doorway but still look casual and nonchalant so he wouldn't know that I'd been waiting for him.

With a plump strawberry in one hand, I lingered by the dessert table for what felt like ages when Dan finally came out with a tray of cake. This was it!

I pretended to almost walk into him and grasped his forearm to balance myself. Hello, muscles. "Sorry, I didn't see you."

He laughed. "It's okay. Do you want a piece of cake?"

"Hmm, it does look good, but I don't know if I should. I don't know if I could handle any more food."

His eyes slid down my dress and he grinned. "You still look good to me."

Cheeks flushing a bit, I smoothed out the invisible wrinkles on my green dress. "I guess I could handle a slice and go to the gym tomorrow to make up for it."

"If you want to work out, I know this really nice jogging path in the park if you're interested."

I . . . was not. I mean, I was fine with working out as long as

I had air-conditioning and didn't sweat too much, but I wasn't going to tell Dan that. "I'd love to. But I don't like to run by myself. It gets lonely."

Moving the cake tray to one arm, Dan reached into his pocket and pulled out his phone. "Why don't you give me your number, and I'll call you the next time I go? You know, so you could have some company."

Victory! With a wide grin, I reached for his phone when Mom suddenly appeared out of nowhere and tugged on my elbow. "Mia! Why don't you and Jake go dance before we leave? Don't you owe him one?"

I pulled my arm away. "Uh, no. Why would I owe him one?"

"Because you two always dance together. Ever since you were kids." Mom wrapped her arm around my shoulders and laughed. "You two make such a cute couple."

"But we're not—"

Dan shoved a cake plate into my hand and backed up. "Uh, I should get back to the kitchen. They're starting to pack the leftover food for the couple to take home."

"Dan, I didn't—" Watching him sprint back into the kitchen, I groaned. "Seriously, Mom? Did you really have to do that?"

She waved her hand like she didn't just embarrass the hell out of me. "It's fine. They're about to do the bouquet toss anyway. You need to get a good spot in the front before all those bridesmaids crowd in."

Oh. My. God. If we were a cartoon, there would literally

be steam coming out of my ears right now. I let out a frustrated groan. "I don't *need* to get a good spot for the bouquet toss just like I don't *need* to dance with Jake. Or talk to him. Or do *anything* with him. You're the one who's forcing me to."

"I just thought—"

"Forget it. You never listen to me anyway." With a scowl, I stalked back to our table and grabbed the opened bottle of cognac in the middle and poured myself a shot. Tossing it back, I gasped a bit as it burned down my throat and then I shoved nearly half of the cake slice into my mouth as a chaser. It was cool and sweet but didn't do anything to cheer me up.

JAKE

MOM AND I WERE just getting ready to leave when Mia tapped on my shoulder. "Could I talk to you for a second?"

Damn it. I was so close to finally getting out of here. "About what?"

Her gaze flickered over my shoulder. "Why don't we dance?"

"Uh, why?"

"Because it's a wedding and that's what people do?" Without waiting for my response, she grabbed my hand and yanked me toward the dance floor. It was still a bit early, so there were only a few people dancing. Mainly kids, their parents, and a couple of drunk adults.

A little girl twirled toward us, and I actually had to tug Mia out of the way so she wouldn't get run over. Surprised by the sudden movement, she stumbled on her heels. Usually when Mia wears heels, she still isn't very tall, but she must have worn super heels today because the top of her head was eye level with me.

She swept her hair over one bare shoulder, and my eyes followed her movement down to her green dress.

I didn't dare look down any farther. Not unless I wanted to get my ass kicked. Instead I focused on her face.

Her left brow was arched slightly higher than the other. The fake lashes she wore framed her dark chocolate eyes, making them look wider than usual. Then my gaze moved down to her pink lips, and I forced myself to look away.

Suddenly, Mia pulled out of my arms as soon as we were out of sight of our moms.

"What are you doing?"

She sat down on the steps next to the stage. Her chin pressed against the palm of her hands. "Honestly, I didn't want to dance. I just didn't want to go home with my mom right now. And I knew the only way she would leave me alone for a few minutes was if I were with you. Could you just stay here for a bit?"

To be honest, I was ready to go home half an hour ago. For some reason, the stupid DJ had been playing every single song that reminded me of Finn. Every song we sang together. Everything he did. It was like a freaking Finn Adler concert.

And the constant reminder in the back of my head that I'd

have to physically see him in a few months only made me more pissed.

But Mia kept staring at me—eyes wide and pleading—and I couldn't say no. God, this was annoying. I leaned against the stairs railing and crossed my arms. "Five minutes."

She nodded and pulled off her heels. "Seriously, though, isn't it kind of ridiculous how long this has been going on? Fifteen years is definitely overkill. We have to do something. Does priesthood seem appealing to you?"

"Not really."

"Yeah, I didn't think so." Mia made a face. "I mean, I've seen your browser history."

What the hell?

"I wasn't being nosy. Not really. I accidentally saw it a few months ago when I was printing something off of your laptop. Plus, I noticed the *video site* that you go on." Her fingers made quotation marks at the word *video site* before turning away with a smirk. "I meant to save it to blackmail you with some-day." She paused. "Damn it, I shouldn't have told you that I knew about it."

My face burned. I didn't know if it was annoyance or embarrassment. Probably a bit of both. Counting to ten, I let out a deep breath. "I think your five minutes of having a human shield is up, so good luck on your ride home."

I tried to walk away, but Mia reached out and grabbed the

side of my pants and continued chattering. "Seriously, if only we could somehow get them to give up on us. And we finally wouldn't have to do everything together. No more rides to school. Summer vacations. Sunday brunches—"

I stopped trying to pull away and stared down at her. "Wait, what did you say?"

"About Sunday brunches?" She pouted. "I mean, I love dim sum, but I'd be willing to give up my shu mais and soup dumplings if it meant that I didn't have to see you all the time."

Barely listening to Mia now, I sat down beside her on the step as my mind raced. She was right. If our moms gave up on us being together, then we wouldn't have to do any more stuff together. Stuff . . . like the cruise vacation this summer.

This was perfect.

The more I thought about it, the more I became obsessed with the idea. I scooted closer to her side. My arm lightly touched hers. "You know what? Screw our moms. I think it's time that we put an end to this. I mean, it's not going to work out between us no matter what they do. So rather break their hearts now than later, right?"

"Yeah, right. And how do you think we're going to do that? Talk to them?" She rolled her eyes. "Because I've tried that. Hundreds of times."

"Really? Hundreds?" My hand pressed against my chest. "I'm kind of honored that you spend that much time talking about me."

"You wouldn't be if you knew what I say about you."

Now I mock clenched my heart. "Ouch, that hurts."

She patted my shoulder. "You're a big boy. You'll survive."

With a laugh, I shook my head. "Too bad we're not dating for real. Then they would really see how much of a train wreck we actually are."

"Seriously. I mean, ew." After a few seconds, Mia's eyes widened thoughtfully. "Actually, why don't we?"

"Why don't we what?"

"You and me. Date."

The hell? Now it was my turn to stare at her. How much did she have to drink? "You want us to date for real? Like for real, for real?"

Mia chewed on her lower lip again, making it puffier and a shade pinker then her top lip. She really had to stop that or her lips were going to fall off someday. "Sort of. Just for two weeks or something. You know, give them what they want and then have the worst breakup of all time."

I don't know if I was just desperate, but everything Mia said made sense. And it was crazy enough to work. "That's not a bad idea."

"I know. I'm so brilliant that I surprise myself sometimes." She smirked. "You know when this is over my mom won't be around to fawn all over you anymore. Can your ego handle it?"

"Well, you know that might be pretty hard. But finally having you out of my life will make it all worthwhile."

She rolled her eyes so far back that I could see the whites of her eyes. "You just reminded me of a million and one reasons why us being together for *real* is such an awful idea."

"Hey, I'm just stating the truth."

Mia stood up so quickly that the ends of her hair almost hit my face. The faint smell of her shampoo drifted over to me. Some kind of sweet fruit and flowers. Lilies? Apples? I took a deep breath but couldn't really figure it out. Would it be weird to ask her? Probably.

I climbed to my feet, too. "So we agree." Reaching out, I grabbed two champagne glasses from a passing waiter and handed one to Mia. I held it up between us. "We're going to *date* so we won't have to *date*. To no more Sunday brunches."

Her eyes twinkled, and she clinked her glass against mine. "And separate dentist appointments."

As I downed the glass, I couldn't help thinking that if this actually worked out, then I'd be free of both Finn and Mia from my life. Two birds with one stone.

What started out as a shitty night just turned into a pretty awesome one.

MIA

MOM'S FINGERTIPS BRUSHED against my forehead. "Are you sure you don't need me to stay home with you? I could make you some soup. How about chao ga?"

Man, chicken congee did sound pretty good. All warm and filling. Especially since this freak cold front blew through overnight and it had been drizzling all day. Still, I mustered up a pathetic little cough and shook my head. "No, you should get dim sum with the Adlers. I'll probably just sleep or something."

"It's actually just Mrs. Adler. Jake suddenly had to work." Her hand froze and she narrowed her eyes at me. "Which seems suspicious now that I think about it. Are you actually sick? Or is this just a ploy to get out of dim sum?"

Crap, was she onto me?

I laughed. "If I *wanted* to get out of something, it wouldn't be something like dim sum. You know my week is screwed up if I don't have my steamed pork buns."

She still looked suspicious, but luckily she pulled away. "All right. Well, I'll be home in two hours or so. Probably going to talk to the florist about the Wilson wedding before I come home. Let me know if you need anything."

I snuggled into my pillow and pulled the blanket up to my chin. "I will. Have fun."

A couple of minutes later, I heard the front door slam shut. I waited at least thirty seconds for her to walk to the car before I jumped up to peek through the blinds. Mom pulled out of the driveway and picked up Mrs. Adler, who was waiting for her on the sidewalk. After they left, Jake popped out of the front door, and my phone immediately buzzed.

Pressing the speaker button, I tossed it on my bed and yanked my baggy T-shirt over my head. "I'm coming out now," I called out before he could say anything. I rummaged in my dresser and grabbed the first shirt I found to pull on, a dark blue tank with ruffles on the hem. I pulled on a gray cardigan. "Don't turn the engine off. I'm literally walking out the door right now."

"Which means it'll be another five minutes."

"Ha. HA. Has anyone ever told you how hilarious you are?" I grabbed the phone before slipping on a pair of sandals. "Because they're lying."

He snorted. "Don't be mad just because you can't appreciate all my awesome qualities."

"Sorry, there was static. Awesome or awful?"

"Now look who has all the jokes. Can you just get out here so we can get going?"

"Fine," I said, just to have the last word, because that was important.

As I slipped out the front door, I made sure to pause to fix my hair right in front of the doorbell. It was pulled into a high ponytail that somehow emphasized my ears. Damn. Still, Dumbo ears were better than having my hair in my face all day. And I didn't need to try too hard to look good for Jake anyway. I tugged on the tendrils around the side of my face to cover my ears for at least a minute before hurrying down the sidewalk.

"What was that for?" Jake asked when I jumped into his car.

"Just making sure my mom saw me leave on the doorbell camera," I said with a grin. "She should get the notification in a minute or two."

"You should have told me. I would have parked closer so she could see you get into my car."

"Don't worry. The range on that camera is pretty good. We could even see people stealing fruit from the house across the street." My mom was so observant that she should have been a spy. If she wanted to, I'm sure she could give James Bond a run for his money.

Her name was Le. Sydney Le.

Jake laughed. "Nice. I turned on the location app on my phone, so now all we have to do is let ourselves get caught by them on our date. Too bad we couldn't just *tell* them that we were dating or something."

Now it was my turn to snort. "Yeah, right. Like they would believe us. At least this way it looks like we tried to keep it a secret."

"True." His fingers gripped the steering wheel as he turned onto the highway. It was still early enough that there were only a few cars on the street. "Just hope this works."

"You and me both."

We didn't say anything else until we got to the park. Jake wanted to go to the movies or something, but I figured it would be harder for our moms to find us there. At least the park was wide open enough that they could spot us no matter which direction they came from. It was just a big open green space with benches around the four sides, and it was so much more romantic than the movies.

Although I didn't plan on the sucky weather. I couldn't help shivering a bit when I got out of the car. With a smirk, Jake tossed me a spare jacket from the back seat of his car. I wanted to refuse it, but the brisk wind made my pride evaporate. I stuffed my arms in and zipped it up practically to my chin.

"So where do you want to hang out for our 'date'?" His fingers rose to make the quotations at the word *date*.

Rolling my eyes, I reached out to grab his hand. Damn, why was his hand so warm in this cold weather? I fought the urge to press it against my freezing face. "We can just sit on the benches—"

"In the rain?"

"The rain will just make everything seem more romantic." My other hand swept my damp hair off of my face. "You know, all soft and dewy. Haven't you ever watched any romantic movies? The kisses in the rain are the best ones."

"Yeah, who doesn't want to make out and drown at the same time? Pneumonia is the best." Suddenly, he cocked his head at me and frowned. "Hold on, we didn't say anything about having to kiss."

Good Lord, it was like we were six, and he was afraid I had cooties again. "Jeez, that was just an example. All we need to do today is act like we don't hate each other when our moms show up. Do you think you'll be able to pull it off, Casanova, or should we just give up now?"

To my surprise, Jake laughed and pulled me closer until the sides of our arms were pressed together. He gave my hand a squeeze. "If that's what it takes for me to finally get you out of my life, then I'll manage."

I sighed, tugging on the end of my ponytail in frustration. Just then I noticed what he was wearing. Or rather *how* he was wearing his clothes. His T-shirt was wrinkled, and his jeans actually had holes in them. Small holes that kind of looked too neat to be natural, but still holes. "It's too bad, too. You got dressed up and everything. Well, actually dressed down. You know, you don't look half-bad like this. You look like a normal teenager."

He smirked a bit before tugging on the collar of his shirt. "Aw, you're making me blush."

"...and now I take it back." I rolled my eyes. Couldn't even compliment him without having his big head get in the way. Still, at least he was trying.

"Why don't we just sit on this bench and enjoy each other's company until our moms show up?"

The bench had a slight sheen from the drizzle, but luckily Jake's jacket was so long that it pretty much covered my butt. I sat down beside Jake and swung my arms back and forth because I didn't know what to do. I forgot that I was still holding Jake's hand, though, so he got yanked along with me.

With his eyes closed, Jake let go of my hand and wrapped his arm around my shoulders until my head was pressed against his side. He smelled like laundry detergent. The fresh-linen kind. Not the one that was heavy and smelled like men's cologne. Just clean. His other hand slightly stroked the side of my arm, making my eyes snap to him. He didn't seem to notice what he was doing, though, so I didn't move away. It felt weird. Not *bad*. Just ... weird. How could I feel his touch through all these layers?

Jake and I pretty much never ever touched each other, much less held hands. I mean, yeah, we always had to sit next to each other, but we made sure not to get too close. Didn't need to spur on the Jakia fan club.

Even though I was used to having Jake around, this was something completely new.

He suddenly stiffened. "Don't look up, but I'm pretty sure our moms just pulled into the parking lot."

I froze. "Really? They must have skipped dim sum and came straight here. What should we do? Should I scoot even closer to you?"

"Any closer and you'll be sitting on my lap. And I don't think that's the impression you should be giving on a first date." His eyebrow rose. "Or do you?"

"Shut up." I automatically punched his chest before I realized what I was doing. Instead, I pretended to stroke it. I scrunched my face up and tried to give Jake a loving look, but to be honest, I probably looked like I was constipated or something. Especially judging by the weird look on his face.

Yeah, this wasn't going well at all. At this rate, our moms would see right through us.

Oh, what the hell. Might as well go for it. I wrapped my hand around his other shoulder and leaned up to give him a kiss on the cheek. Or at least I tried. He bent his head at the same time and our lips touched. Well, barely grazed one another before I jerked away in shock and he ended up kissing my nose. Right smack on the tip where I slathered practically a whole bottle of zit cream this morning to cover up the bump.

Oh my God, this was mortifying on so many levels. I'm pretty sure if we weren't sitting on this bench, I would have just melted away to the ground with embarrassment.

Thankfully, I was saved from saying anything because a bright flash of lightning streaked across the sky. Loud thunder soon followed it.

"I think that's our cue for the date to be over." Jake grabbed my hand. "Come on."

Hand in hand, we raced to the car. My sandals smacked against the ground, making the back of my legs wet. Reaching the parking lot, we each dove into the car just as a huge sheet of rain came pouring down.

Tiny beads of rain clung to the top of his head. Not enough to make it wet, just kind of glistening as his hair curled around the nape of his neck. Jake reached into the glove compartment and handed me a couple of napkins to dry myself off first.

I dabbed at my arms and the back of my legs. "So . . . do you think that was enough?"

Before he could say anything, both of our phones started to buzz. One glance and I could see Mom's picture on the screen. Jake laughed and waved his still ringing phone at me. The word *Mom* flashed on his screen. "I guess this answers your question. No turning back now."

"So . . . should we pick up?"

To my surprise, he shook his head and shoved the phone back into his pocket. His eyes twinkled with amusement. "Nah. Let's let them suffer for a bit longer."

I grinned. "You know, I hate to admit this, but you're not so bad after all. If you were like this more often growing up, then you would have actually been fun to be around."

He gave me a pointed look. "Thanks, but don't start doodling my name in your notebook or anything. Remember, we're doing this to get out of each other's lives."

Rolling my eyes, I dropped the phone back into my purse and cranked up the heat. "And now I remember *exactly* why we're doing this. But thanks for the reminder."

Jake snorted and adjusted one of his air vents to point at me so the warm air blasted in my direction. Instead of saying thanks, I leaned back into my seat and closed my eyes.

It was probably a good idea to rest now so I could face Mom and Mrs. Adler later. Because having to pretend that I was in love with Jake was going to take every ounce of energy I had.

JAKE

OUR MOMS WERE BOTH waiting for us at Mia's house when we came home. Actually on the front porch, even though it was storming. I don't know how the hell they made it home before we did, though, since they were driving behind us practically the entire time. They stood side by side with their arms crossed.

"Okay, it's now or never," Mia announced as soon as we parked in her driveway. Even though her voice was confident, her left leg bounced up and down like a basketball. "Remember, we have to make it convincing, or they won't believe us. We only have one shot at this so don't screw it up."

"I know." She had been saying the same thing over and over on the whole ride home. Along with her "tips" on how to be convincing.

After she didn't move for a few moments, I leaned over and pressed the button to release her seat belt. "Come on. The sooner we get this over with, the sooner we can break up and be free. Hey, you might even have time to find a date for prom if this works out."

Her eyes brightened. "That's true. I didn't even think of that. What are we waiting for?"

Before I could respond, she hopped out of the car and ran around the front toward her house. I climbed out and chased after her. We were both pretty much drenched by the time we got onto the porch. With their arms linked together, Mom and Mrs. Le blocked the doorway.

"Hi, Mom. I didn't expect to see you here." I tried to act surprised as I crossed and uncrossed my arms. Everything I did felt awkward, though, so I ended up stuffing my hands in my pockets.

"Of course you didn't. Especially since you told me that you were going to be working all day," Mom said with a raised eyebrow.

"And you," Mrs. Le said, pointing at Mia. "I thought you said you were sick. Why are you out with Jake?"

Mia let out a forced laugh. "What? No, I'm not out with Jake. We were just . . . I mean—"

"We saw you two at the park."

"I—" Mia stopped and blinked at her. "You . . . you did? What exactly did you see?"

"Quite a lot," her mom said with a nod. "Almost everything. But we want to hear it from you."

Mia and I exchanged looks, and I tried to keep my face calm.

"Since you saw everything then I guess you guys already know." I reached out and grabbed Mia's hand. It was cold and a little wet. My fingers laced through hers and held on tightly. "The secret's out. We're together now."

I don't know what I was expecting with our announcement. Tears of joy. Applause. Anything but the suspicious looks they shot us. Well, Mrs. Le looked suspicious. Mom just looked confused.

"I don't understand. When did this start?" Mom asked with a frown. "Yesterday you two still hated each other."

"We did." Mia shot me a side-glance. "But something happened at the wedding last night when we danced. It was different. Something clicked. So we actually snuck out last night to meet up and just started talking. And . . . I don't know. It just happened."

"Today was supposed to be our official first date," I continued with our rehearsed story. "But we didn't want to tell you guys in case this relationship ended up not working out. I mean, everything still feels too new. So I lied about having to work, and Mia pretended to be sick."

"We just wanted some time to ourselves to see what *this* was. Whether it was just the one time or if it's something real." Mia motioned between the two of us. Blinking innocently, she turned to face her mom. "But how did you know we were at the park anyway?"

"Oh, I just—" Looking guilty, Mrs. Le swept her hair over her shoulder and laughed. "We just happened to be passing by while we ran errands, and we saw Jake's car. Totally coincidental. I swear."

"Totally," Mom echoed. "Wait, so you're together now? Like you two are actually dating?" Her hands clasped together in front of her face. "For real?"

With a bright smile, I let go of Mia's hand to wrap my arm around her shoulders. "For real. You were right about her, Mom. She's wonderful."

Mom beamed, but Mrs. Le slowly shook her head. "Something just doesn't make sense."

I let out a frustrated sigh that I turned into a cough. "Could we just go inside before Mia gets sick for real?"

"Oh, right."

Our moms turned and trooped inside. We followed a few steps behind.

"What now?" I hissed at Mia under my breath as I kicked off my wet shoes to put in the corner.

"Just play it cool." Mia pulled away and ruffled her fingers through my wet hair. "I'm going to grab a couple of towels from Mom's room so we can dry off," she said loudly before rushing off.

"Wait—"

Great. She ditched me. Now I was stuck with both moms.

With no other choice, I followed them into the kitchen and sat down on a counter stool. They both sat down in the chairs facing me, and I couldn't help feeling like I was about to be punished.

Luckily, Mia appeared at the doorway and handed me a towel before dabbing the top of her head with the other one. "Here."

"Thanks." Instead of using it, though, I took a corner and wiped at the droplets clinging on Mia's nose and cheeks. She froze for a second or two and lifted her face until I was done. I gave her a tiny wink before rubbing my hair with the towel.

The expression on her face softened a bit, and Mrs. Le leaned back into her chair. "Okay, now I think we should start from the beginning. . . ."

It took a while longer for her to believe that we were actually dating. A lot longer than I expected. And our moms wanted more details. Thank God we worked out our story last night and in the car. They made us go over it several times as though trying to catch us in a lie.

Mia and I squeezed closer and closer together as though it would help convince them. I was getting pretty tired of the interrogation.

When the news finally sank in, it was like lightning struck.

Their expressions totally changed, and they actually started squealing.

For a split second, I felt guilty at the happy expression on Mom's face, but Mia jabbed her elbow in my side like she knew what I was thinking. I couldn't help it, though. I had never lied to Mom before. Well, occasionally a white lie here and there, but that was it.

When the cheering finally stopped, Mia wrapped both arms around my waist and leaned against my side. "Well, now that everything is out in the open, you guys should go eat. We're going to continue our date. Probably hang out in my room for a bit until the rain stops before we catch a movie and grab a bite to eat."

Maybe it was the lightning flash, but I swear Mrs. Le's smile faltered a little bit. "Just you two? Alone? Why don't you come eat with us?"

"I don't really—"

With a small smirk, Mom patted Mrs. Le's arm. "Sydney, you know the kids don't want to hang out with their moms. Especially *now*."

Her face cleared. "Oh, that's right. Well, you kids have fun."

I reached behind my back and laced my fingers through Mia's. Her fingers were tiny and smooth. "We'll see you guys later."

Knowing that our moms were probably still watching us, we stayed plastered together up the stairs like we were in a three-legged race. It wasn't until we were safely in her room that she let out a deep breath and dropped my hand. "That's weird. Did you see that?"

"See what?"

"Usually my mom would practically push us into a room together, yet now that we're dating, she seemed kind of reluctant for you to come into my room." She eyed me from head to toe with a raised brow. "Do you look hornier or something today? Like she's worried that you'll take advantage of little innocent me?"

Scoffing, I fell back onto her bed, bouncing a couple of times as I made myself comfortable. The bedsprings squeaked a bit. Loudly. I half expected one of our moms to come bursting in. "Whatever. If anything, she's probably worried that your messy room will scare me away before this relationship even starts. Seriously, when was the last time you cleaned in here?"

Her lips pursed together as she thought about it. "Last June."

"Oh. God." I tried to get up, but Mia shoved me back down and swung her legs onto my lap—practically sitting on top of me—to trap me. "If your mom walked in right now, she'd know that I'm not the horny one."

"Please, like you could ever make me think about you like *that*."

Was that a challenge? "That makes two of us. I am surprised that they believed us, though."

"Yeah, especially with that sad excuse for a kiss." She smacked her hand against my shoulder. "Why were you trying to kiss my ear? Is that your secret fetish?"

"Ouch. I was trying to kiss your *cheek*. It wasn't my fault that you turned your face at the last second."

Her face scrunched up. "I had to turn away to gag when you called me 'honey.'"

I let out a short laugh. "This plan is doomed to fail before we even get started. God, how are we ever going to convince them that we're really dating?"

"Not with that kind of attitude! Now, what are we eating later?" With a frown, Mia grabbed a pillow and smacked the top of my head.

When did she get so abusive? I yanked it away before she could hit me again. "I'm not hungry."

"Great, because I wasn't going to eat with you anyway." Her sigh was so heavy that I felt like I could practically see it. "We just need to figure out what we had in case our moms ask."

She was right. Now I felt stupid. "Oh, right. Good thinking. How about pizza?"

"I had pizza twice this week."

"Which would suck if we were *actually* eating pizza. But we're not."

Mia wrinkled her nose. "Still, we have to be believable, and my mom knows that I would never eat pizza three times a week. How about ramen? Or sushi!"

I threw my hands up. "Fine, whatever. You can decide on the pretend food we're going to have for dinner and just text me about it later."

Again, I tried to leave, but she planted her foot firmly on my chest and pushed me back down. "You can't leave yet. They're still home."

"Well, what are we going to do until then?"

"It is Sunday . . ."

There was a small smile on her lips as her fingertips tapped together like Mr. Burns from *The Simpsons*. My forehead scrunched together as her smile grew even wider. What the hell was she—

It finally clicked when she leaned back to open her night-stand and pulled out a couple of those Korean face-mask thingies that made you look like a ghost. "No. No. NO."

"Yes. Yes. YES." Her hand smoothed them all out on the bedspread like a colorful pack of cards. "Now which one do you want? I have moisturizing ones with aloe and cucumber. Some collagen wrinkle-free ones. Or even this one with a picture of a baby's foot. I don't really know what it does since all the words are in Korean, but I assume it's something good. Look how soft and glowing that baby's toes are!"

Picking up her feet, I shoved her off of my lap, and she flopped backward with a squeal. I grabbed the baby-foot mask from the bed and pointed it at her like a sword. "I'm not doing this."

Her eyes widened innocently. "What? It's not like it's your first time."

"One. Time," I nearly growled. "And we swore that we would never talk about it again."

"And now it's about to be two times that we will never talk about again. Come on, pretty boy. You have to keep up your looks if you're going to be dating me. By the way . . ." She knelt and faced me. Her elbows braced against my shoulder as she leaned forward and gave me a quick peck on the cheek. "For future reference, that's what a kiss on the cheek is supposed to be."

Not sure why, but the kiss took me by surprise. I stared at Mia for a moment before finally pushing her away. "Fine, you win. I'll do it if it means you'll stop kissing me." I ripped open a package before slapping the mask on my face. The strip on my nose wiggled as I sighed.

Mia let out an identical sigh and poked at the moist edges around my chin to smooth them out. "Ah, we've only been dating a few hours, and the magic is already gone."

"You're talking like there was ever any magic in the first place," I said with a snort. I climbed next to her and laid down on her pillow. My eyes closed to dismiss her. "Let's just get this over with."

"True." She laughed and laid down next to me on the bed. The top of her head was pressed against my forearm.

Now, I would never admit this to Mia, but the cool sheet

actually felt good against my face. Especially because I felt hot all of a sudden. Plus, it smelled good.

Cracking one eye open, I peeked over at Mia and almost jumped off the bed. My mask was so wet that it slid off my face. Instead of a plain white mask like mine, hers looked like a panda. With black circles around her eyes and a snout. Her hair was still tied up, but she also had on a pink headband that pushed up the top of her hair like it was a spiky pineapple.

It took all the effort I had not to laugh and wake her up. With a smirk, I slowly opened my phone and snapped a picture of her. Just for insurance, in case she tried to pull anything else on me in the future.

After a couple of shots, I laid back down and closed my eyes.

Now that the first step of our plan was over, I felt relieved. Like the huge boulder was finally off my shoulders. To be honest, this morning I was pretty sure we were going to screw it up. But somehow, we actually got our moms to believe us. And that was definitely the hardest part.

Mia yawned and snuggled a little closer into my side. The side of her head brushed against my shoulder. I lifted my arm to move away, but she just nestled into my chest and let out a soft sigh. I thought she might have woken up, but a few seconds later, her breathing was slow and even again.

I'd forgotten that Mia was a snuggler. Ever since we were kids. During naptime in kindergarten, she would always roll from her mat onto mine. Every single time. It didn't matter if I was on her right or her left side. After five minutes, she'd be pressed against my arm.

Funny how she never rolled onto anyone else's mat.

With a sigh, I wrapped my arm around her shoulder and leaned my cheek against the top of her head. Her hair tickled my nose, but I just blew the few strands away and closed my eyes.

For the first time in two years, I fell asleep immediately.

MIA

IT WAS ONLY NOON, but I already felt like I had been in school *forever*. I stifled another yawn while Todd Kim, my bio partner, chatted about the guinea pig dissection we were supposed to do next week. Not exactly the best topic to talk about before lunch, but Todd was one of the top students in the class and because most of my biology knowledge basically came from *Grey's Anatomy*, I pretty much needed all the help I could get.

Rubbing my eyes, I stopped short and blinked so rapidly that my contacts moved. At first, I thought I was imagining things, but there was Mom coming out of the office with a tan envelope in her hand. Aly was right behind her, probably having just finished up her free period filing.

"Okay, okay, I got it. Dissection. Heart. Little veins. I'll see you tomorrow!" I shooed him away midsentence. "Mom! What are you—what are you doing here?"

"I just came by to talk to Mrs. Martin, your adviser. She needed my expertise to plan your prom and senior events next year." She clenched the strap of her tote bag. "What about you? Where's Jake? I was hoping to catch you in the cafeteria to say hi."

My mind was a blank. "Jake? He's . . ."

"Jake's waiting for us to meet him for lunch." Aly interrupted, poking her head in between us. "Right, Mia?"

I shot her a grateful smile. "Yeah, but I'll tell him to meet us up here instead."

"That's okay. I can go downstairs—"

There was no way I could let her go down to the cafeteria. It was one thing to pretend to be dating at home, but I wasn't going to be all lovey-dovey with Jake in front of the entire school.

"No! No. I'll just get him." I pushed her to sit on the bench right by the office door. "Stay right here. Aly actually has something she wanted to ask you."

Her wide blue eyes stared at me. "I do? I mean, I do! Yes. Lots and lots of questions about . . . stuff."

"So just stay here and talk while I get Jake." Before Mom could try to follow me, I spun on my heel and ran off. My hand dug my phone out of my pocket and I called Jake, but he didn't pick up. Where the heck was he?

I sprinted upstairs past Jake's locker, but he wasn't there. Still redialing his number, I ran down two flights of stairs toward the cafeteria on the first floor. Why the heck did his locker have to be on the third floor anyway?!

My heart pounded in my chest, and I bent over—hands on my knees—as I struggled to catch my breath. God, I felt like I was going to be sick. This was why I never joined the track team despite Coach Hill's best efforts. Apparently, he just couldn't understand why someone with my "muscular legs" didn't run.

Maybe this was how I was going to die. When I had so much unfinished business. I still needed to go to college. I still needed to meet Lee Jong-suk, my Korean love. And I still needed to return that movie to Redbox before they fined me.

Scanning the cafeteria, I spotted Jake sitting with Rose in the far back corner. I sprinted over to his side and grabbed the bottle of iced tea from his hand.

"Mia, what the hell—?"

Holding up a finger, I opened the bottle and basically guzzled nearly half the bottle before breathing deeply. "Why didn't you pick up your phone?! Forget it. You need to come with me. My mom—" My eyes darted over to Rose. I was pretty sure that Jake probably told her about our deal. I mean, they were best friends, but I wasn't positive. "You just have to follow me."

His face was all scrunched up, but he eventually got up. I wrapped a hand around his elbow and steered him toward the exit.

"Uh, do you want to let me know what's going on or do you just want to keep acting like a crazy person?"

"My mom came to drop off some forms at the office and wanted to say hi. I didn't want her to go into the cafeteria to look for us. Especially with everyone—Mom!" I nearly smacked into her right outside the doorway. "What are you—I thought I told you to wait for us by the office."

Aly stood a couple of steps behind her. Both hands rose in a shrug, and she mouthed the word *sorry* over and over.

"It's fine. I parked by the cafeteria anyway. I didn't want you guys to have to come all the way upstairs to meet me." Mom beamed at us standing side by side. "Look at the two of you. You're just so cute together."

Jake pinched my left cheek. "I'm not sure about me, but I won't deny that Mia is cute."

Gritting my teeth to hold in the groan from his cheesiness, I plastered a dorky smile on my face and patted his shoulder. "Oh, you, stop it."

"I'll never stop it." This time he squeezed both of my cheeks. His eyes sparkled with laughter. "Don't know how I was able to resist your charms all these years."

Gah, he was enjoying this way too much. Thankfully, Mom couldn't see my face as I glared at him. After a minute or two, I couldn't take it anymore and dug my heel into his foot until he grunted and let go of me.

Two could play this game. I reached up and patted his

cheek. Hard enough that it could almost be a slap, but I made sure to keep a loving expression on my face the entire time. "All those video games over the years must have made you blind."

"Maybe." His jaw was tight, but he kept the smile up before kissing the top of my head. "So I have to stop by my locker to get something, but I'll see you later in the cafeteria. Bye, Mrs. Le. It's nice seeing you."

"Bye, Jake."

As he walked away, behind Mom's back, he turned and pointed his index and middle fingers at himself before pointing at me with a threatening expression. I snorted. Mom turned slightly to look behind her, but I pulled her in for a tight hug. "Thanks again for stopping by, Mom. Maybe next time you can sign me out and we could go get lunch."

"Maybe I'll bring Mrs. Adler. It could be a group date!" She clapped her hands together with glee.

I forced a bright smile on my face. "Sounds great!"

She patted me on the head twice and tucked a stray hair behind my ear before she turned away to leave. And even then, she would turn her head back every few seconds to wave like a kid. As crazy as she was, Mom could be cute sometimes.

"That was fun. Your mom should come around more often," Aly said with a grin when Mom was finally gone.

I groaned. "Not unless you want me to have a heart attack."

———————

"TWENTY-FIVE. TWENTY-SIX." I shuffled through the scripts again, but no matter how many times I counted, there was one extra. I was sure I only punched in twenty-five copies. Maybe the machine just decided to spit out another one for fun. I picked up a pack to staple.

"Hey, Mia?"

"Yeah?" I looked over and nearly toppled out of my seat. "Ben! What are you—how—I mean, HI!" Why did I sound like such a blabbering idiot? I cleared my throat and tried again. A little deeper. Sexier. "I mean, hey . . . man. What's up?"

He slid down onto the stool beside me. His chin was propped on his hand and he gazed at me. "I was just surprised to see someone else here this early."

My hand brushed a strand of hair behind my ear, and I tried to look cool even though my stomach was in knots. "Oh. I just wanted to make sure everything was set up before rehearsal, that's all."

Ben let out a low whistle. "I don't know what Daniel would do without you. Are you planning to help out next year, too? Maybe try out for a part or something?"

I snorted. "Yeah, right. Like I could ever do that."

"Why not?" He leaned forward like he was confiding a secret. "I think you would be awesome."

"Huh?" Were there gold flecks in his eyes or was it just my imagination? Something about Ben made me feel like the eleven-year-old me in Victoria's Secret for the first time.

Embarrassed, awkward, and unsure if I was even supposed to be here.

His beautiful brown eyes were looking at me so intently that it took me a few minutes to realize that he was done talking. "Sorry, what did you say?"

This time he did laugh, but I didn't mind because it made his eyes almost sparkle. "I was just saying that you should try out sometime. Being onstage is amazing. And to perform in front of a live audience? Seriously, I can't even describe how that feels."

Focus, Mia. Focus on his words. Maybe if I just concentrated on the wood grain on the table, my mind wouldn't be mush anymore. "I wish I could. To be onstage. Maybe on Broadway someday. That's the dream."

"Mine, too." His elbow nudged my arm. "You might as well start practicing now."

I glanced over at the stage and let out a little sigh. If only it were so easy. "I don't know if you've noticed, but you kind of have to have talent to do that sort of thing."

"And?"

"And I don't?"

Ben laughed again. Louder this time. "How do you know until you've tried? I could even run the lines with you sometime if you want. Help you practice."

I blinked at him in shock. "Now?"

His left hand reached up, and he rubbed the back of his

neck. "Yeah, now. Or maybe over the weekend we could meet up. Get some coffee while we're at it."

Weekend, coffee—hold on . . . was he asking me out?!?

"I hate coffee," I blurted out without thinking. "No, wait, I mean, yeah, that sounds really great!"

Oops. Should I have played it cool first? Was it too late to backtrack and be coy? I brushed my hair behind my ear and shrugged, attempting to seem nonchalant. "If you don't mind helping me. I'd love to."

His grin was wide and covered half of his face. "Great. I'll text you later tonight."

"Okay, but how do you . . . is this your way of asking for my number?"

"I don't know." Ben crossed his arms and leaned toward me again. My heartbeat immediately went into hyperdrive the closer he got. "Depends if you think I'm being smooth or lame."

Why was it so hard to breathe? "Smooth. Definitely smooth."

His lips twitched into another smile. "Then I was definitely asking for your number."

After I punched my number into his phone, Ben picked up the rest of the scripts I had left and stapled them with such efficiency and ease that I almost swooned. I'm pretty sure I would have swooned no matter what he did. He just made everything look so *cool*. After he was done, he stacked them together and handed the stapler back to me with a wink as he got up. "It's a date, then."

"Date," I repeated again like the village idiot. Gah. My cheeks hurt from smiling so hard.

It took a minute or two, but the word *date* suddenly sank into my muddled brain and snapped me out of my stupor. Uh, date? Damn it. What was I thinking? I couldn't go on a date. Especially when I was supposed to be dating Jake. Mom would freak out.

Although *technically* it wasn't a date date. We would be rehearsing. Over coffee. Or something.

My hand smacked my forehead. Over and over again. Thank God Ben was already gone.

Maybe I should cancel. I didn't want to. God, I didn't want to. It wasn't every day that the guy of your dreams asked you out on a date. Even though it wasn't *really* a date.

My forehead hit the surface of the table with a loud thud.

Still this may be the only chance I ever got to go on a date with someone like Ben so I'd be an idiot to throw it away.

I glanced down at the stapler in my hand and sank back into my chair with a sigh. My hands grasped the stapler to my chest like it was a bouquet of roses.

A goofy grin crossed my face. Lyndon came in and gave me a funny look, but I didn't blame her. I knew I looked crazy, but I didn't mind one bit.

Because at least I wasn't an idiot.

JAKE

EVEN THOUGH I HAD texted Mia ahead of time to let her know that I was coming over, she still looked surprised when I showed up at her front door. It was only six o'clock, but she was already in her pajamas—a stretchy white tank and baggy striped purple pants that were way too long for her. They covered her feet, and I could barely see her toes peeping out. Her hair was tied up on the top of her head like a messy hat.

She braced both hands on either side of the doorway like she was a guard blocking it. "What are you doing here?"

"Our date? I texted you about it. . . ."

"Oh. My phone was dead when I got home so I plugged it in. I guess I forgot to check it."

I nodded. "Guess so. So now what?"

Her head leaned against the doorframe. "My mom's not even home, though, so seems like a waste of time."

"Well, I already told *my* mom that I was coming over, so . . ."

Letting out a heavy sigh, Mia finally straightened up. "Fine, you can stay here for a bit as long as you don't bother me."

"Gee, I'll try my best." I followed her into the house to the kitchen, but not before taking off my shoes.

After I grabbed a bottle of water from the fridge, I started to ask Mia where her mom was but something stopped me. Leaning forward until my face was a few inches from Mia's face, I wiped at her neck with my index finger. "Why's your neck wet?"

She blinked wide eyes at me for a few seconds before letting out a slow deep breath. "I just got out of the shower when you came over."

"Then why isn't your hair wet?"

Her hand flew to the top of her head. "I don't wash my hair every day. I usually just put dry shampoo on."

"What is—?" Making a face, I backed up a few steps. "Never mind. Don't need to know. I'll just keep my distance from now on."

Mia rolled her eyes. "Is this you not bothering me? Because you're not doing a very good job."

"That was before I knew about your weird hygiene habits." I downed the rest of the water bottle and moved to throw it away by the sink when something outside caught my eye. "I've always wondered, why did your mom keep the tiny house that Frank was working on?"

She peered out the window with me. Both hands braced against the edge of the sink as she leaned forward. "I think Mom didn't have the heart to tear it down after they broke up. He was a good guy."

"I liked him." Truth was, I barely remembered the guy. I just remembered him hanging around when we were seven. Probably couldn't pick him out of a lineup now, but I remembered that he always brought us ice cream. "Do you mind if we check it out?"

Mia shrugged. "Why not? I haven't been in there in ages."

Once we were in the yard, she fell into step beside me. Our strides matched even though my legs were way longer. But her pace was always a little faster than everyone else. Like she didn't have any time to waste getting to the next place.

I hopped on the skinny wooden makeshift porch and pulled the door open to peek inside. I knew it was a tiny house, but this was a lot smaller than I remembered. Like this was literally *tiny*. It was basically the size of my room at home.

Mia followed me inside and stopped by the little area beside the door that was marked off with bright blue tape. "Remember this was where he planned to have a couch that would convert into a twin bed? For guests. Although I have no idea why you would invite guests over in such a tiny place."

I hopped onto the metallic counter and leaned against the wall. With my right leg bent, I rested my arm on my knee. "Does your mom miss him?"

She traced the windowsill with her fingertips. "I think she does. She never said it out loud, but sometimes I'd catch her watching HGTV with a distracted look on her face like she's thinking about him. Well, except for when she's drooling over those guys on *Property Brothers*."

"My mom does that, too. The drooling part, not missing Frank." I glanced around the kitchen. "I really don't remember this house being this *small*. Not for you, though, since you were a shrimp. Still are actually."

Her upper lip twitched. "Well, it's not like you're some sort of giant. You're not that tall, either."

"Still a lot taller than you," I retorted.

"That's not anything to brag about." Placing both of her hands on the countertop, she hopped up to sit, too. Or at least she tried to. It was a little high so she bounced up and down a few times like a crazed bunny until I reached out to help. One of my hands clasped around her arm while the other wrapped around her waist as I lifted her up. "Thanks."

We both sat there swinging our legs in silence. It was . . . kind of nice. I don't know if it was the sentimental memories in this house or because she was less annoying today, but I didn't really mind having to hang out with her. My hand traced a couple of purple smear marks on the cabinet door beside my head. "Remember how we used to pick raspberries from my mom's garden and 'make' our own jam?"

She rolled her eyes. "I remember that. Mom and Frank were so pissed when they couldn't scrub those marks off."

They were. My butt was sore just remembering that time. I shifted back and forth before realizing that Mia was doing the same thing. Our eyes met, and we both started laughing. I didn't really know why. I mean, it wasn't *that* funny, but it just felt like a time to laugh.

The counter we were sitting on was kind of small so we were kind of smushed together. Just then I noticed that my hand was still around her waist. Well, not *exactly* around her waist. My arm was behind her back, but I could still feel her waist pressed against my hand. My hand against her hip. Almost on her butt.

Shit.

"Hold on a second. You have dust in your hair." Mia reached out and ruffled the top of my hair with both hands.

At first I froze, but after a little while, I bent my head a bit so it would be easier for her. Every movement she made, every brush of her fingertips, sent shivers down my neck.

When she finally stopped, I tilted my head and peered over at her. Our faces were only a few inches apart now, and I could see the dark pupils in her brown eyes. The tiny mole on the left side of her chin.

My breath suddenly got caught in my throat as if I had been running around the block, but I hadn't moved in the past five minutes. Was this what a heart attack felt like? That didn't explain why my hands were suddenly all clammy. And it especially didn't explain why I couldn't stop staring at Mia's face. Or her parted lips that looked really soft and inviting all of a sudden.

Okay, I've always *known* that Mia was pretty. I wasn't blind. Greg even had a small crush on Mia that he tried to hide, but it was obvious from the way he flexed whenever she was around. Yet this was the first time *I* ever thought that she was *pretty*. If that made any sense.

I don't know.

She pulled back, away from me. "That's better. I didn't want you to freak out because you got a little dirty."

"Thanks." Looking down, my gaze fell on a tiny smiley face drawn on her hand with a blue pen. "What's this?"

"Huh?" She glanced down and rubbed the mark. "I was a little tired at rehearsal today, and this guy drew on my hand to cheer me up."

"That's weird. Didn't you say you just got out of the shower?"

"I guess I didn't scrub hard enough." She tilted her head down, but I could have sworn she was blushing or something. But why the heck would she be blushing over a smiley face?

"Let's go back inside." With pink cheeks, Mia hopped off the counter. She fumbled with the doorknob a bit, and I had to reach around her to open the door. "Uh, thanks," she said. "I have homework to do. It is still a school night."

Man, she wasn't very subtle in wanting to get rid of me. "Sure, see you later. I'll just go home through the side gate." I walked her back to the house before turning to the side. "Hey, Mia?"

She turned around. "Yeah?"

"Only a week and a half left."

"Left . . . ?"

"Until our breakup. And then we'll never have to put up with each other again."

A brief smile crossed her face. "Can't wait. Bye, Jake."

As I walked back to my house, those words kept running through my head. A week and a half. Eleven more days. Then it would finally be over and we would have our freedom back.

MIA

THE LUNCH BELL RANG just as I grabbed my history book from my locker to stuff into my book bag. I was supposed to meet up with Jake and Aly by the bench outside the gym to discuss the rest of our dating plan. So far, it looked like Mom and Mrs. Adler believed us, but we had to keep the momentum going before we broke up next weekend.

Just as I was zipping up my bag, there was a knock on my locker door. I glanced up at Ben's beaming smile, and I automatically grinned in response. "Ben! Hey, what are you doing here?"

"I was about to get some pizza with my friends and just wanted to see if you'd like me to bring you back any," he said, leaning his shoulder against the locker beside mine. A lock of dark blond hair fell forward over his forehead. "Pepperoni? Supreme? Four cheeses?"

With a soft laugh, I shook my head. "I'm okay, but thanks."

"Maybe next time, then."

I expected him to leave, but he fell into step beside me as we headed toward the stairwell. Our arms swung back and forth between us. My stomach twisted in knots at how close he was. Our hands were inches from touching. "So, uh, are you excited about opening night in a few weeks?"

Ben chuckled. "Yeah, but it's not like I'll even be onstage. I'm just an understudy. Not unless Leon comes down with the flu or something."

"Hey, it can happen." I twisted the strap of my bag around my index finger. "You would be better at the role than Leon anyway. In fact, you'd probably be doing the audience a favor if you took over."

"Thanks. But don't let Leon hear you say that," he whispered as he leaned in closer to me. My heart went into overdrive. "Sometimes he can be a bigger diva than Lyndon."

"Oh, I've heard his complaining across the theater. But don't worry, I won't say it again even if it's true." I pretended to zip my lips, which made him laugh again.

Before we knew it, we reached the first-floor hallway by the cafeteria. Disappointed, I wished I had thought ahead to take the long way down here.

He cocked his head toward the cafeteria. "You're not going in?"

"Uh, no. I'm supposed to meet Aly and—" I started to say Jake's name but stopped for some reason. "Just some other friends by the gym. We're working on a project."

"Oh, good luck, then. I'll see you at rehearsal tomorrow." He gave my arm a tiny squeeze before leaving.

I had to hold my breath to not let my excited squeals escape. But nothing stopped me from practically skipping outside to the gym. Aly and Jake were already there, waiting for me. She was perched on one side with her legs tucked beneath her while Jake sat on the other side munching on a bag of chips.

As soon as I sat down between them, Jake surrendered his half-eaten bag of Cheetos to me. "What took you so long?"

"Uh, I'm barely two minutes late. Give me a break. You know how Mr. Tiller likes to go on and on even when the bell rings." I popped a chip in my mouth. "So, what are you guys talking about?"

"Jake was just telling me about the dates you had so far. At least his version." Aly's eyes twinkled as she smirked at me. "You didn't tell me about your kiss."

I snorted. "The nose kiss? Because it wasn't even worth mentioning."

"I don't know. A kiss is still a kiss, you know."

Jake rolled his eyes. "She's just mad because I wouldn't agree with her kisses-in-the-rain idea."

I hit his arm. "They are the best!"

Aly pursed her lips together and nodded. "I have to agree. They really are the best. So romantic and sweet . . ."

"See?"

"Oh my God, and what makes you two experts?" Jake asked with a raised eyebrow.

"K-dramas," Aly and I both responded in unison.

With a loud sigh, he stared up at the sky. "This is going to be a long two weeks."

"One and a half," I corrected. "Which, by the way, we still have a lot of work to do before we break up next weekend."

"What do you mean? I thought all we had to do now was go on a couple more fake dates, and we'll be done."

Aly gave me a sympathetic look. "No wonder you told me that you needed my help. He's pretty much useless."

"I know, right?" Ignoring his loud "Hey!" I pulled out a piece of paper and pen to jot down notes while I explained everything to him. "We can't just break up after a couple of dates, because our moms will think this was just a fling. And they might hope that we would get back together in the future."

"So . . . ?"

Jeez, it would probably be easier talking to a toddler. "So we have to convince them that these two weeks are serious and when we break up, it's for good. No ifs, maybes, or buts about it. We're done."

"It would probably help if you two got hot and heavy while you were at it," Aly added with a grin.

Now it was my turn to roll my eyes as I held in a gag. "I don't think that's necessary."

"Okay, maybe not exactly hot and heavy, but you *are* going to have to kiss for real. Rain or not." She crossed her arms over her chest. "No one is going to believe you're actually dating if you don't kiss at least once."

Jake and I gave each other weary looks before I caved and wrote down the word *kiss* in my notes. "Fine, we'll kiss in front of Mom and Mrs. Adler . . . one of these days. Now let's move onto more enjoyable things, like how we're going to break up."

"You mean we can't just break up, either?" His left eyebrow rose. "Why can't anything be simple with you?"

"Because simple is forgettable. And we want our breakup to make an impact." I tapped the top of my pen against my left cheek. "So, any ideas?"

"Well, I guess the whole rich guy and poor girl trope won't work. Neither will the opposing families trope." Aly chewed on her lower lip. "You guys are like the opposite of that one."

I racked my brain to think of the other various reasons why couples broke up in the dramas. "No medical conditions, either. No one's getting cancer or amnesia."

"And you're not forced to move away from each other. Either for school or supernatural intergalactic reasons."

My hand patted my chest, and I pretended to swoon back on Aly's shoulder. "That reminds me, we should really rewatch

My Love from the Star again. I need another dose of Kim Soo-hyun to survive."

She nodded. "We should. I miss his alien hotness."

Jake shot horrified looks at the both of us. "Seriously, why do you guys watch these things again? They sound ridiculous."

"It may sound ridiculous, but that doesn't mean it's not also amazing." Crumbling up the empty Cheetos bag, I sat upright and turned to face him. "Well, how do you think we should break up?"

"I don't know. A huge fight? Basically show why we never should have gotten together in the first place."

Aly looked pensive as she twirled a strand of hair between her fingers. "The whole opposites don't always attract. It's simple, but it could work. Maybe we could work in a past first-love angle, too. Who was your first crush, Jake?"

He shifted back and forth in his seat. "How am I supposed to remember that?"

I didn't say anything. Nor did I look at Jake or Aly. I just kept looking straight ahead at the sophomore guys tossing a football back and forth and prayed that Aly wouldn't ask me.

Jake may not remember his first crush, but I definitely did. And it was awkward because he was sitting right next to me.

I didn't even remember exactly when or how I started liking him. It was before we turned seven because we were still friends. I think maybe even that summer before second grade.

I would wait around all morning for Mrs. Adler to bring him over. Not just to have someone to play video games with and eat Cup Noodles for lunch, but because I liked seeing him. Hanging out with him.

It didn't last too long, though. Not after we realized the reason our moms kept pushing us together. That was like tossing a pail of water on my burning crush. But he was still my first crush.

"I think Jake is right. We could just have a huge blowout over everything that annoys us about each other," I said, changing the subject before Aly could ask me about my crush. "That would probably be the most realistic plan anyway."

She looked disappointed. "I guess. It's the more boring one, though, but it's up to you guys. Your fake relationship. Your breakup. At least after next week, you'll be able to date whoever you want, Mia. And Jake . . ." She hesitated. "Why are you doing this again?"

That was a good question. I never really stopped to think about why Jake was going along with this plan. I mean, we were both sick and tired of getting shoved together by our moms, but honestly, it's been like this for a while. The wedding was the last straw for me, but I didn't know what made Jake so desperate.

Jake's dark eyes flitted back and forth before he shrugged. "I just thought it was time, that's all."

"But—"

With a cough, I nudged Aly's side with my elbow to get her to stop. I may not know *why* he was doing this, but I could tell when something was really bothering him. Especially when his left leg would start bouncing up and down like an earthquake.

"So, it should be easy enough to get into a fight next weekend," I said to cover up the uncomfortable silence. "I mean, we've got a thousand things we could fight about."

"A thousand and one," Jake joked. His leg immediately stopped bouncing. "So, I guess that's it?"

"Yeah, I guess so."

Now it was Aly's turn to nudge my side. "What about . . ." She tapped on the paper on my lap with the single word *kiss* on it.

Jake and I exchanged looks and immediately jumped to our feet. "We'll figure that out later. Lunch is almost over anyway." I pretended to glance at my phone.

"I still have to meet up with Rose about some work stuff." He was already backing away from us like he was afraid he'd catch our cooties or something. "I'll see you after class."

Aly waited until Jake left before she stood up and wrapped an arm around my shoulders. "If just talking about kissing gets you two this rattled, I have no idea how you're going to survive the rest of the week being all lovey-dovey in front of your moms."

I let out a heavy sigh but didn't disagree with her. I was still busy watching Jake as he disappeared into the building. There was a nagging feeling in my gut, and I half wanted to follow him to make sure he was okay.

Instead, I brushed it off and turned to Aly. "Let's just grab something from the cafeteria before lunch period is over."

MIA

SO IF $X^3 + Y^3 = (XY)$...

I stared at the problem in my calculus book, but my eyes kept flickering over to the extra script next to my book bag. And my phone right next to it. Ben hadn't called or texted me yet, although it was only six o'clock. He still had plenty of time to call. Plenty of time.

I shook my head and tried to concentrate on the problem instead. So far, I had been stuck on this particular one for the past twenty minutes.

No matter how much I worked through the equation, my answer ended up longer and more complicated than the actual problem. Which made absolutely no sense. Plus, why would I ever need to solve equations like this in the real world? It wouldn't help me get a job or land a rich husband.

Okay, the rich husband part was just a joke. I would never

date a guy because he was rich. Then again, if a rich guy suddenly landed in my lap and we fell in love, then that would be all right. Rich and handsome. And possibly could sing or cook a mean pan of lasagna.

But either way, I'm sure he would not care if I could solve for x or y or whatever the answer to this stupid problem was.

Okay, I needed a break before my head exploded both from waiting for Ben and from calculus. Going into the kitchen, I grabbed a can of Sprite from the fridge. The save-the-date card from my cousin Trang's wedding fluttered off, but I caught it with one hand and put it on the table.

Mom was sitting by the counter munching on a piece of Korean pear as she shopped for clothes on her tablet. Without looking up at me, she slid the plate in my direction. "How's your homework going?"

"Confusing. Stressful. And kind of feels like I'm getting an ulcer." Even though I was still stuffed from the bag of chips I had inhaled when I came home from school, the pears looked so crisp and juicy that I couldn't help grabbing one. Dropping onto the stool next to her, I inhaled another pear slice within a blink of an eye. "Would you mind if I just quit school and became a professional poker player for a living?"

"Sure, but you're definitely *not* going to be living here if you do that. I assume you'll be living in your penthouse in Vegas."

"Of course. You know me so well."

She finally glanced over at me. "If that's your plan, though,

I think you should learn how to bluff. You've never been a very good liar."

That's what you think.

I leaned forward on my elbows, and my feet kicked against the legs of my stool. "Maybe I'll just win the lottery instead."

"Yeah, that definitely sounds more reasonable. What does Jake think of your new career aspirations?"

"He'll probably say I'm crazy."

Mom laughed and pushed her tablet away. "That does sound like him before you were dating. How are things going between you two?"

"We're . . . good." I glanced up at the clock on the wall and jumped up. "Actually, I'm supposed to meet him in front for a date right now. We talked about watching an early movie before dinner."

"That's nice. I'll walk you over to their house. Mrs. Adler and I are going to a yoga class tonight to focus on our *chi*." She wrapped an arm around my shoulders. "I'm so glad that you're both finally together. Have I told you that?"

Only a million times a day. I forced a smile on my face. "Me too. I always thought we were too different, but sometimes different isn't that bad."

She beamed. "I've been telling you that for ages! Like yin and yang. It's about time you finally listened to me about how perfect you two are."

I fought the urge to roll my eyes as she locked up. I couldn't wait for all of this to blow up so that I could finally rub it in *her* face how wrong she was. That thought cheered me up as we walked toward the street.

"What's that?" Mom pointed at my car.

It took me a few seconds to figure out what she was pointing at because there was a glare coming off my windshield. But as I got closer to my car, I saw a folded white note and a couple of daisies tucked beneath my windshield wiper. "I don't know. . . ."

Careful not to get too close because I was allergic to daisies, I grabbed the note and opened it.

Saw these at the grocery store and thought of you. Looking forward to running lines with you tomorrow.

—Ben

A stupid smile crossed my face even though my nose started itching like crazy and I had to take a step back from my car. How did he know exactly where I lived? Although, our town was so small, it wasn't that surprising. Everyone lived within ten minutes of one another. But before this week, I was surprised that he even noticed me, much less knew where I lived.

I mean, I could tell he was flirting with me earlier today, but this went so beyond just casual flirting. This was right into the "I like you" phase. I tapped the note against the palm of my hand. Should I call him to thank him or maybe send him a cutesy text? Or maybe—

"Who are the flowers from?"

"Huh?" I looked up at my mom staring expectantly at me. The fluttery feelings melted away into panic. For a second, I had forgotten she was here.

Crap. I couldn't tell her that these were from Ben. Especially since I was still in the honeymoon phase with Jake.

"I . . . uh . . ." Apparently my stupid brain decided that *now* would be the perfect time to take a break. Like during my Spanish final last year. *Mi estupido cerebro.* I knew that now because I had to retake the Spanish class this past summer. "Oh, *these* flowers. They're from . . . Jake!"

"Yeah?"

I swung around just as Jake and his mom came up our driveway. God, what were the chances that they would show up *now*?

"Jake!" I rushed over to his side and gave him a quick hug. "I just got your note and flowers. You're so sweet. You know you could have just given them to me during our date."

"I—flowers?" His eyes narrowed in confusion as he looked back and forth between the car, my mom, and me.

Thinking quickly, I pulled his head down to give him a kiss. Just a soft one on the lips before murmuring, "Just go with it."

Jake stayed frozen like that for another second or two, our lips just barely touching, before pulling away from me. He looped his arm around my shoulders and squeezed me. "I just wanted to surprise you before our date."

Letting out a sigh of relief, I glanced over at our moms watching us like we were a Lifetime movie. Their hands were clasped together in front of their chests, and they were practically leaning against each other.

"I didn't know you had such a romantic son, Lily," Mom said with a nudge in Mrs. Adler's side. "Although you really should have remembered about Mia's allergy to daisies."

Mrs. Adler gasped. "How could you forget?"

"I . . ." Jake scratched at the side of his neck and laughed. "I remembered something about Mia and daisies so I thought that was her favorite flower. The allergy part must have slipped my mind."

I patted his arm. "It's okay. You still get points for trying."

Mom nodded and waved us along. "No harm done. It's the thought that matters. We'll get rid of the flowers for you. Go have fun on your date."

"Maybe we could drop them off with Jess down the street," Mrs. Adler said as she grabbed the flowers from my car. "She's been feeling so down since her dog died."

"That's a good idea. I just baked some lemon cookies, too . . ."

As soon as our moms went into the house, I pulled away from Jake and let out a deep sigh. "Thanks for helping me out."

"No problem." He shoved his hands in his pocket. "Who are the flowers really from?"

I glanced down at the note and slid it into my bag. "Oh, just someone in the theater group. It's nothing."

He let out a low whistle. "I don't know. Dropping off flowers at your house. That's a lot of trouble for just nothing. I guess this means you'll be going to prom after all."

My cheeks felt flushed. "We'll see. It's still early."

"Uh-huh. Well, remember to tell Theater Boy about your allergies before he gets you a daisy corsage or something." His voice had a mocking tone to it as he crossed his arms and leaned against the trunk of my car.

Instead of responding, I shrugged and started walking down the driveway. Jake had to spin on his heels to follow me.

I don't know why, but it felt weird to talk to Jake about Ben. Maybe it was because I still didn't really know what Ben and I were now, much less what we would be when prom came around. Plus, it might not even go anywhere, so it was pretty hard to explain. Especially to someone who was supposed to be my boyfriend. And someone I kissed from time to time. Even if it was all fake.

We didn't say anything else as we crossed the street to his car. Jake suddenly quickened his footsteps to pass me up and got to the driver side before I even reached the sidewalk. Instead of getting in, though, he just stood there watching me with a funny look on his face.

Once I got to the passenger side, Jake opened his door. But he still didn't get in. "Mia?"

"Yeah?"

He cleared his throat. "I remembered that you were allergic to daisies. That time in fourth grade when we had the field trip to the nature center. Remember? You started sneezing so badly in the greenhouse that I had to sit with you in the courtyard while Mrs. Conrad called your mom to come get you."

I stared at him. "I forgot all about that. You even went home with us that day."

He shrugged. "You were all sad about having to go home early. I figured you'd cry less if I missed the field trip with you." The tips of his ears were a tad bit pinker than usual. "Anyway, I just wanted you to know that I did remember."

I was still confused, but for some reason, this seemed important to Jake, so I nodded. Plus, I was actually a little touched that he remembered something from so long ago. "Thanks."

He flashed me a smile and hopped into the car. I climbed in after him. Jake immediately flicked on the radio and cranked the volume up before pulling out of the driveway.

We didn't talk the entire ten-minute drive to the movie theater. I couldn't help glancing over at him every few seconds. I don't know why. My eyes kept looking over at him as if they were pulled by a magnet no matter how hard I tried to look away. Studying him. From his dark, slightly curly hair to his jawline. The little mole on the bottom of his right earlobe. The way he drummed against the steering wheel, in tune with every song that came onto the radio.

He seemed different, yet somehow exactly the same. But I just couldn't figure out what it was.

JAKE

I WAS LATE picking up Mia. Again. Damn, she was going to kill me. Might as well pick out my tombstone now.

She wasn't waiting in the front lobby when I got there, so I went through the theater back door. It was so dark that I thought it was empty at first. There was only one spotlight focused on the center of the stage. I was halfway up the steps when suddenly I spotted her.

Her eyes were bright with concentration as she lifted her head and sang a verse. I could barely hear the words because she kept stopping to curse to herself. Her dark hair swirled around her face, and she had to stop twice to brush it away. The spotlight beamed right over her, illuminating her like she was some type of illusion. A vision.

She said something again, a bit louder this time, and twirled, but she stumbled on her own feet. I leaped forward to help her, but someone else caught her instead. Some guy who was standing partly in the shadows on the stage. Mia must have known him because she just gripped his arms and *giggled*.

Yes, giggled. In the fifteen years that we've known each other, the only time I've ever heard her giggle was when she had her wisdom teeth taken out and was high on the drugs. That was when she also planned an escape route to live on Mars when the zombies took over the world.

Who the hell was this girl? And why was she still in his arms, leaning on him?

I cleared my throat, and Mia and the guy jumped apart. She squinted her eyes in my direction. "Jake?"

"Hey, I just came to pick you up." I glanced over at the other guy. "I thought the rehearsal would be done by now."

"Oh, it's been over for a while. Ben was just offering to, hmm, help me practice some lines. He's in the musical." She coughed and wrung her hands as if she was being punished. "Ben, this is Jake."

He held out his hand, and I reluctantly shook it so I wouldn't look like a douche. "Sorry, I didn't mean to keep your girlfriend from you."

"She's—"

"Oh, no, Jake isn't my boyfriend," Mia explained. "He's just . . . a neighbor. We've known each other for years. I mean, our moms wished we would be together, but that's definitely *never* going to happen. We're just pretending to date for now. But we're not dating each other for real. Or anyone."

Ben laughed.

"In other words, we're not dating," I said.

"Good to know." Ben lightly touched Mia's arm. "I've got to go, but I'll see you at the next rehearsal?"

"Yeah, of course." She giggled again, and my stomach clenched for no reason. She continued waving at him until he left before turning to me. The happy look on her face instantly disappeared. "What?"

"Nothing. I was just waiting for you to finish drooling after him. That's all."

Her mouth dropped open. "I wasn't—I didn't."

"Whatever. Better call someone to wipe the stage before they slip on your drool." I hopped off the stage and landed in the center aisle with a loud thump. "Is that Theater Boy?"

"Yes . . ."

"Why'd you tell him all that stuff about us and our moms anyway? I thought you didn't want anybody to know."

She slipped off the edge of the stage and hurried after me. "I don't know. It just slipped out. I guess Ben is different."

My eyes narrowed. "What does that mean?"

Instead of answering, Mia just shrugged.

What kind of response was that? I don't know why it irritated me so much, but it did. We promised that we weren't going to tell anyone except Aly and Rose about our plan so we wouldn't get caught. Hell, I didn't even tell Greg about it although that was mainly because he was a blabbermouth. Still, he's more trustworthy than some strange theater guy.

"Why are you bothering to practice lines anyway?" I asked with a scowl. "You're not even in the musical."

Surprised by my angry tone, Mia gave me a funny look as we left through the back door. "I just—I just wanted to try out some of the scenes in the musical. Why are you so pissed?"

"I'm not pissed. I just think that it seems like a waste of everyone's time to stay after rehearsal to run lines. Mine. Ben's. All for nothing."

Her mouth silently opened and closed a few times. "Well, I couldn't do anything during rehearsal while the stage was occupied. With the actual actors rehearsing. Duh. And Ben didn't mind. *He* offered to help *me*."

I didn't know why I was lashing out at her, but the words just poured out of my mouth. "I just don't understand. You photocopy stuff and run errands for people. Why are you onstage in the first place?"

Something I said struck a nerve. The confused expression on her face melted away into anger. Mia slammed her hand against the hood of my car. Her eyes flashed at me. "I'm sorry for wanting to try something new for a change. And for your information, I photocopy and do *stuff* because that's all I *can* do. I mean, let's face it. I can't sing. I can't dance. I know that. I'm not delusional. But at least I'm trying."

It was like everything that Mia had pent up inside of her was gushing out. Like a Pandora's box. And I didn't know how to stop it. Okay, I was the one who started this—poked the bear, stirred the hive, whatever—but I didn't expect *this*. "Okay, I'm sorry—"

But she wasn't done. "And I know it's pathetic. You don't have to tell me that. All I can do is watch Lyndon practice her lines and dream that someday I'll get to be a lead, too. But at least I *try* to go for my dream. Which is more than what I can say about you."

I held up my hands in surrender. "Hold on, what do I have to do with this?"

"Because you're being stupid. You *can* do something with your music, but you don't. You're just throwing it away. I *hate* dumb people like you who waste away their talent." Her finger jabbed the air with each statement, and I almost felt the force. "Which if you ask me, makes you the bigger idiot."

Was she serious? My hands pressed against the hood of the car as I leaned toward her. "*I'm* an idiot?"

Bracing both palms on the car, Mia mimicked my stance until she was nearly right in my face. "All I know is that if I had *half* of the talent that you do, I wouldn't waste it like an idiot. Maybe you should just get on with your life like he has."

My jaw clenched. She didn't specifically say his name, but we both knew who she was talking about. Like she had a right to talk about him. Mia was the only one who was around when

Finn left. The only one who saw how abandoned I was. Hell, she even came over to be with me so I wouldn't be lonely. I didn't ask her to, but she did it anyway. Just sat there watching TV with me until dinnertime. For weeks. She understood what I went through. Understood me.

Or at least I *thought* she did.

"Gee. So far in the past two minutes, you've called me stupid, dumb, and an idiot." I counted off each point on my hand. "Anything else you want to add?"

Her chin rose a couple of inches, and she walked backward. "Yeah. I'm taking the bus."

"Fine with me."

We both stared at each other for a few seconds before turning away at the same time. I hopped into the car and jammed my key into the ignition. Without looking over at her, I peeled out of the parking lot.

I didn't go far, though. As angry as I was, I wasn't stupid. No matter what Mia said, I couldn't just ditch her here alone at night. Then I really would be an ass. But I sure as hell wasn't going back for her, either.

So I ended up parking on the side street for twenty minutes, waiting for the bus to pull into the bus stop. Mia just sat on the bench with her arms crossed as she scowled at everyone who drove by. Once, two dudes came by to talk to her, but before I could go over to help, she said something that sent them running.

Despite the fact that I was still pissed at her, a smile jerked to my lips, and I wished I were close enough to hear what she said to chase them off. As annoying as Mia was, she was pretty badass when she wanted to be. Her only good quality.

I followed the bus home, making sure to stay a few cars away. Luckily, there was a stop right at the corner of our street so Mia was off the bus and walking up her driveway within minutes. She dug her phone out of her pocket as she walked. Probably calling *Ben* to make plans for their next *practice*.

My left hand smacked against the steering wheel before I turned off the engine. Whatever. We only had a little over a week left of this relationship anyway. After that, Mia could do whatever she wanted with Theater Boy. It wasn't any of my business.

When I got out of the car, I slammed the door so hard that the bang echoed down the quiet street. A startled stray cat screeched and jumped off the neighbor's porch to run down the sidewalk. A couple of dogs down the street started barking, too.

All the noise was probably bothering the neighbors, but I didn't care. At this point, I didn't really care about anything. Including Mia and What's His Name.

MIA

MRS. LACEY SCRIBBLED a series of numbers on the board. The longer she wrote, the more squiggly her handwriting got. "Now remember to look over these problems from chapter fourteen for the test next week. Especially focus on the . . ."

I knew I should be copying this down, but I could barely pay attention to anything Mrs. Lacey said. The fight Jake and I had last night kept drifting in and out of my head.

For the first time in my life, I'll admit that I actually was a brat. A Brat with a capital *B*. I took it too far with Jake. I know I did.

God, I don't know why I brought up Finn like that. That was low. Like I ripped the Band-Aid off his wound and punched it. I knew that was the way to hurt Jake the most.

He was devastated when Finn left. Just retreated into a quiet shell. I'd never seen him like that before. It took months for him to get back to normal. And even now there were times when I would catch him looking over his shoulder as though he expected Finn to still be there. And then a brief flash of sadness would cross his face.

But it stung when Jake pointed out that I had no right being in the theater. I was already embarrassed enough after practicing with Ben. He tried to be nice, but I caught him wincing once or twice when I tried to hit a high note. Then Jake had to come barging in with his insults. Like he's so high and mighty—

Never mind. Take a deep breath, Mia, and just let it go.

I did some breathing exercises, trying my best to channel Yoda before I apologized to Jake. Well, not *apologize* exactly, because he was the one who started it. But I didn't help it, either, so I figured I would extend the olive branch.

Still, not sure how convincing I would be if I were glaring at him the whole time. Even if it was partially his fault.

I was getting worked up again. Gritting my teeth together, I shook my head to try to calm down. What were those Lamaze breathing things again? *Hee, hee, hoo.* Or was it three *hees* and a *hoo*?

Great, now I sounded like a freaking Dr. Seuss book.

The bell rang, and Mrs. Lacey started to wipe the board clean. "Okay, remember I'll be out for the next few days. I have to go to my cousin's wedding in Boston, but I left plenty of assignments behind for the substitute teacher so don't think you can goof off. You'll have the test when I get back so work hard."

Crap. I'd drifted off again. I glanced around to find someone to get the study assignment from, but half of the class was already herding out the door.

Thankfully I was able to grab the problems' numbers from Mindy Lee right before she ran off to PE. After tucking my binder in my bag, I hurried down the hall toward Jake's locker. He wasn't there yet, so I ducked behind the classroom door nearby.

Letting out a deep breath, I rehearsed what I was going to say to Jake when he finally showed up. Keep things light. Maybe open up with a joke or two. The one about the dentist and doctor who walked into a bar was pretty funny. Or maybe—

A hand clasped onto my shoulder hard, and I jumped nearly a foot into the air. My arms waved around. "I know karate, so back off!"

"Mia?"

Not even sure when I squeezed my eyes shut, I blinked and dropped my arm. "Oh, hi, Rose."

She laughed and leaned against the wall beside me. Her manicured nails tapped against the edge of her English book. "What are you doing?"

Blinking rapidly, I attempted to look nonchalant. "Just, you know, hanging out."

"Behind a door?" With a half smirk, Rose shot a knowing

glance toward Jake's locker. "If you were looking for Jake, you just missed him."

Now it was my turn to laugh, although it sounded pretty half-hearted. I tugged at the strap of my book bag. "No, why would you think I'm looking for him? I'm just reading the flyers on the bulletin board. Dance team's audition is next week, you know. But, hmm, if I were looking for him, do you know where he went?"

"Not sure. I just saw him drive off at lunch."

Whoa, Jake cut school? He's never done that before. Something must have really been bothering him. My chest felt heavy with guilt. I hoped it wasn't because of the Finn thing.

Rose poked my arm. "Can I ask you something?"

"Uh, okay."

Her blue eyes sparkled with amusement. "Tell me the truth . . . do you really know karate?"

"Sure, I do! I have a black belt." My hands rose, and I pretended to karate chop the air. "From Macy's. Michael Kors's fall collection. Sixty percent off."

She laughed and linked her arm through mine, tugging me toward the door. "I've been meaning to ask you, did Jake ever tell you anything about the music festival next week? It's for new and up-and-coming musicians."

"And?"

"And he's just being an idiot about the whole thing."

I snorted. "Typical Jake."

"Basically." Rose rolled her eyes. "I'm friends with Kathy, the coordinator, and was able to get him a spot performing. The problem is I don't know if he's actually serious about giving up music or if he's just being stubborn."

A group of overeager freshmen came running down the hall, and I moved out of the way, pulling Rose toward the windows with me. "What do you want me to do?"

"I need you to go to his room and snoop around. Find traces of new music or anything." She let out a deep breath. "I would do it myself, but he's basically banned Greg and me from coming over because we've been bugging him so much about the festival. Plus, since you two are 'dating,' it should be easy for you to get in."

"I could, but I don't know . . ."

"Please?" Leaning her elbow on the windowsill, she propped her chin on the palm of her hand. "I tried to ask Jake a bunch of times, but he's just so stupid and stubborn."

"Seriously, he never gives in to anything." I coughed and tugged on the end of my ponytail. "Well, sometimes he does when I beg him to. Even if it means driving across town to buy a new pot of orchids that I accidentally let die even after I swore to my mom that I'd take care of it."

The edges of Rose's lips quivered, but she attempted to look serious. "Even though you're insulting him, that basically sounds like a compliment."

"It's not. I'm just . . . stating the truth. That's all."

"Uh-huh." Her lips pursed like she wanted to say something, but she just shook her head. "I have to go find Greg, but call me later if you find anything in his room. And thanks so much for helping."

"No problem. Wait a minute, I didn't say I'd help—"

"Too late! No take backs!" She practically ran down the hall, mowing down a couple of kids like she was on the football field. "Lunch is on me! Thanks again."

Gah, I was already worried about how to apologize to Jake without actually having to apologize, and now I had to sneak into his room and basically invade his privacy. Maybe I should just apologize later after all . . . for the crime I was about to commit.

IT ACTUALLY WASN'T that hard to sneak into his house because I already had a spare key from Mom. We were always running back and forth between each other's houses. Lots of times Mom and Mrs. Adler sent us back and forth just as an excuse to see each other. Like we needed strawberries at four in the afternoon on a Saturday.

No one was home, so I just let myself in and went straight to Jake's room. The door was slightly ajar and squeaked when I came in. Even though I knew I was alone, I couldn't help wincing at the loud sound.

His room was super tidy as usual. There was nothing on the

ground. His shoes were stacked in the corner beside his book-case, which had all the books lined up neatly with the spine sticking up in the right direction. Even his bed was made like a display at Bed Bath & Beyond. My room was the complete opposite. My bookcase at home was filled with books, maga-zines, and a bunch of bobby pins and gum wrappers. Plus, my bed hadn't been made in a month.

The only thing on his desk was his laptop, lid open. How and where would I even find out if Jake had any new music? I doubted he'd have anything written anywhere. And if he did, he'd probably saved it on his laptop.

Holding my breath, I turned it on, but the password prompt popped up. Crap. What could his password be? I tried his and Mrs. Adler's birthdays, but neither worked. I tried Finn's birth-day and even "Adler Brothers," but those still didn't work. Gah. Only two more tries left.

I half-heartedly snooped around his desk and bookcase for clues, but I was pretty much ready to give up. It could be any-thing. His favorite movie. His secret crush. A nickname.

Just then a picture slid out from between a biology text-book and the first *Lord of the Rings* book. I caught it before it hit the ground and flipped it over. To my surprise, it was a pic-ture of Jake and me on Halloween when we were six. Mom and Mrs. Adler made us dress up as Thing 1 and Thing 2. They took a hundred pictures that night and kept calling us the Dynamic Duo.

Why would he keep this picture?

Chewing on my lower lip, I glanced over at the laptop. A nickname . . . there's no way.

With no other ideas, I sat back in his desk chair and typed the words *DynamicDuo* into his laptop and boom! I was in.

With a whoop, I clicked on his browser, but before I could start snooping, Jake's mail inbox popped up. I blinked at the long list of unopened emails from Finn. Jeez, how many emails did Finn send him? The page went on forever. Almost one every week for a year. In between the occasional emails from school.

I didn't even know that they were still in touch. I don't think anyone did. Well, if this could even be considered being in touch.

One thing was for sure, Finn was dying to be back in Jake's life. Except now Jake was the one who was keeping him away. But maybe that wasn't the right thing to do. After all, they were brothers. Family isn't exactly something you can avoid forever.

Maybe . . . he just needed someone to help nudge him into doing the right thing. Someone who knew that *this* was what he needed no matter what he said. In my heart, I knew that he needed to see Finn again. Just ignoring him wouldn't help anyone. After all, they were brothers.

As I chewed on my thumbnail and debated what to do, it

was like Finn's emails were glowing, almost pulsating, and I couldn't look away. I just couldn't leave and do nothing now.

He'd be pissed at me if I butted in, though. Really pissed. Probably wouldn't talk to me again for a while. If ever again. Then again, since we were planning to get out of each other's lives anyway, I guess I was the right person for the job. The only person.

Before I lost my nerve, I snapped a picture of Finn's email address and shoved my phone into my pocket. But when I started opening his folders, there was the sound of a car coming up the driveway. I peered out the window and saw Mrs. Adler parking the car.

Time was up. I shut off the laptop and came out of Jake's room just as Mrs. Adler came into the house. She jumped when she saw me, and her hand flew to her chest. "Oh my God, Mia. You scared me."

"Sorry, I just wanted to drop off . . ." My mind whirled in overdrive. "Jake's sweatshirt. He lent it to me the other day, and I washed it for him."

"Oh, well, that's sweet of you. Do you want to hang out until he comes home from work? I think it'll just be another half an hour or so. I could cook dinner for all of us."

I was already backing toward the front door. "No, I'm good. I have to meet up with Aly. Still have tons of stuff I have to do for school tomorrow. I'll see you soon, though!"

"But—"

As I slipped out the door and ran across the street, one thing kept floating around in my head. With or without the music, Rose owed me a heck of a good lunch for all this trouble.

JAKE

I HAD JUST FINISHED raking the leaves in the front lawn when a navy Accord pulled up in front of Mia's house. Ben popped out and strolled up the Les' walkway like he owned the place.

Damn it. If Mia's mom was home, then our cover was blown.

Dropping the rake, I raced across the street and almost plowed into Ben on the porch. My hand grabbed his wrist just before he rang the doorbell. "Hey, man, what are you doing?"

Ben jerked his hand back. "Oh, hey, Jake. I just wanted to see how Mia was. She wasn't at rehearsal today."

"I think she had to do something with her mom."

"Oh, all right." His eyes flickered down at my hand still gripping his wrist. "Uh, you think you could let me go now?"

Crap, I was still holding his hand. "Sorry." I dropped it like a hot potato. "Anyway, Mia probably won't be home for a while."

"Oh. Maybe I should have called first."

I crossed my arms as I eyed Ben. "Yeah, you should have. Especially since our moms think we're dating. Remember?"

He smacked his forehead. "Crap. I completely forgot about that."

"Uh-huh." Even though he was a few inches taller than me, I straightened up so I wouldn't have to look up at him. "But I'll let her know that you stopped by."

"That's okay. I can just text her later."

"Right, because you have her number." 'Course he could tell her himself. He didn't need me. I was an idiot. "I need to get back to my chores. Before it gets too dark."

Getting my hint, he shoved his hands in his pockets and walked backward toward his car. I half hoped he'd trip on a rock or something. "Oh, yeah, thanks for letting me know about Mia. And it's nice seeing you again. Uh, maybe we should all hang out sometime."

Thankfully, neither one of us seemed excited with that idea.

"Yeah, yeah, sure. Sometime." I didn't leave the Les' yard until his car pulled away from the curb and drove down the street. "Hopefully not anytime soon, though."

AFTER MY SHOWER, I rubbed the edge of the towel against my head and peered out the window at the Les' house. Mia's room was still dark. It had been dark all day actually.

Not that I looked over that often. I wasn't a stalker or something. Just observant.

Where was she, though? Maybe Ben ended up calling her, and she snuck out to see him. Not that I cared. I just worried about her getting into trouble with her mom. Both of our moms.

Or maybe—

Just then, a bright meteor shot across the sky, and an idea lit up in my head. A quick search online later and I grinned. Ah, I knew exactly where Mia was right now.

Grabbing a couple of orange cream Popsicles from the freezer, I snuck out the side door so Mom wouldn't notice and hurried over to the Les' house. The backyard gate was locked, but I just slipped through a loose board on the left side. Mrs. Le swore to fix it every year; she never did.

There in the corner of the backyard, I could see the outline of Mia's body perched on top of the tiny house's deck. She leaned back on her forearms while she stared up at the sky, searching for a meteor. Right where I knew she would be.

Seeing a meteor was number six on her bucket list. Right after attending Hogwarts for real and before zip-lining through the Amazon forest. Let's just say she hasn't been able to cross off much yet.

I coughed until Mia noticed me. It took a little while. "See anything good yet?"

Mia gaped. "How did you know I'd be out here?"

I pointed at the sky. "There's a meteor shower tonight. Where else would you be?"

"But how did you . . ." She scowled. "Wait, don't tell me that you already spotted one."

"Nah, just saw an article about it online," I lied so she wouldn't freak out. I pulled out the Popsicles and held them up like a peace offering. "So could I come up there? I come bearing gifts."

Her lips pursed for a moment. "Okay. But only because I'm starving. These meteors are taking their sweet time."

Handing over the ice cream, I climbed the metal ladder on the side of the house and sank down to sit beside her. The entire "deck" was pretty spacious. Probably about seven feet all around. There was enough room for both of us to stretch out if we wanted to. "You might have to stay out here until morning again. Think you can make it?"

Already licking one of the popsicles, Mia patted at a pillow and a lumpy blue comforter beside her leg. "I've got it covered. I'm determined to cross something off the list this year if it's the last thing I do."

"This is a lot easier than flying to the Amazon to zip-line through the forest." I took the other ice cream from her and bit down. Smooth and icy. And a little bit tart. Mom made these fresh with oranges she bought just the other day. "So how are things going between you and Ben?"

Her head jerked up. "What?"

Damn, real slick, Jake. I didn't mean to burst out with that right away. I wanted to casually bring it up. Slip it in the conversation. Guess there was no recovering now. "It's just . . . he stopped by earlier."

"Yeah, I know. He called me."

"Oh, so you already talked to him." I nodded to myself even though my stomach rumbled uncomfortably. "So what's going on between you two? Are you dating?"

Her cheeks flushed. "We're . . . getting to know each other. He's nice."

Nice? Girl Scouts were nice. Getting extra butter on your popcorn was nice. Did that mean she *didn't* like him? Or it meant that she *did*? And why did I care so much? I don't know why this was so important to me. I just . . . wanted to know.

Mia didn't say anything else and continued slurping her ice cream. Completely absorbed in licking the melted drops running down her hand, she barely paid any attention to me. Just like when we were kids. It was sort of nice to see that some things didn't change.

We were quiet only for a few minutes, but it stretched and felt like an hour. Even the wind rustling through the leaves was too loud. I could feel her eyes looking over at me, but every time I looked at her, she'd look away. I think we were both very aware of the fact that this was the first time we'd been alone since our fight. I know I was.

What should I do? Should I bring it up? Never mention it again?

To be honest, I was a fan of option two, but our fight kept racing through my mind the past few days. Poking at me like an annoying thorn in my side.

Finally, I couldn't stand it anymore. "Listen . . . that day—"

"I'm sorry," she burst out. Her cheeks were flushed in the moonlight, but she cleared her throat and said it again. "I'm sorry about what I said. You know, about you and . . . Finn. And the whole music thing. I was being a jerk."

I expected my stomach to clench up like it always did when someone mentioned Finn's name, but it didn't. "It's fine. And I'm sorry about all the theater stuff. I didn't mean to . . ."

Mia waved her hand. "Don't worry about it. You were angry. I was pretty pissed, too. Let's just call a truce and forget about it, okay?"

"Okay, but just so you know, I was wrong. You can do whatever you want. In fact, I can picture your name in Broadway lights someday." I motioned a sign on the night sky above us. "Big and bright."

"You're delusional." With a laugh, she wrapped her arms around her legs. Her chin cradled perfectly in the nook between her knees. "But kind of sweet sometimes, I guess."

I wanted to argue with her. I wasn't delusional. I really did think she was capable of anything. There was no one like Mia anywhere.

"Let me ask you something." Her eyes lowered to our feet as she traced the wood grain. "If you could talk to Finn, right now, and say anything you want, what would you say?"

Her question caught me off guard. What would I say to him? Yell at him? Curse him out? I spent so much of the past two years trying to forget I had a brother that I honestly didn't know how I would talk to him now.

Finn was someone I used to talk to every day of my life until I was fifteen. Someone I sang with and posted videos on YouTube with. He was the only person who understood how important music was to me. To both of us. That it was a way to release our feelings. Especially when we couldn't figure something out. And it made us happy. I wasn't as good of a singer as Finn, but I did like to write songs. Finn even offered to sing anything I wrote. But he never had a chance to before he left.

Our three thousand subscribers knew his voice. Yet now he was like a stranger. I didn't even know if I could remember what he sounded like. Did he have a raspy voice? Did he sound like me? Did he stutter?

That was stupid. I knew he didn't stutter.

As though she could sense my confusion, Mia's voice softened as she lightly touched my shoulder. "I'm just saying . . . if you miss him at all, maybe you should consider giving him a chance to make things right."

I reached out to push her hand off, but I ended up clasping

it for a second, squeezing it, before letting go. "He doesn't deserve a second chance."

"Everyone deserves a second chance. I love your brother. Heck, I wish he could be *my* brother, except I also think he's kind of hot so that would be weird. Like *Game of Thrones* type of ickiness. Maybe he could be a distant cousin. . . ."

She trailed off, and her face had a faraway look. Not wanting to know what freaky fantasies she was having about Finn, I snapped my fingers in front of her face. "Focus."

"Oh, sorry." Mia suddenly reached out and held my face between her hands. Startled, I automatically jerked my head back, but her grip was both soft and tight at the same time. And she didn't let me move an inch. Man, she could be damn strong when she wanted to be. This was coming from the same girl who could never drag her own luggage through the airport.

Her brown eyes were dark and sparkled a bit in the moonlight. "You're brothers. You love each other. And you're going to have to work this out sooner or later. Might as well be now."

She made it sound so simple. We're brothers, so we'll work it out somehow. But this wasn't a sitcom that would resolve itself in half an hour. Nothing about any of this was simple at all. Just thinking about seeing him again made my whole body tense up and my head hurt. I didn't know how I was going to suffer through the cruise trip if this breakup didn't work out.

"How could you love someone who's never around?" I joked. Half joked. I was kind of serious.

Even if I *did* want to forgive him—and I'm not saying that I did—I didn't even know how to start. I spent so long hating him, ignoring him, that I didn't know how to fix it. Bury the hatchet. Mend the rift. Whatever.

"You just do. Because they're your family." Finally, she let go and leaned forward until she was staring right into my face. I could count her lashes if I wanted to. Kiss her again if I wanted to.

Which I didn't. I don't know why that thought suddenly popped in my head.

"You kind of don't have a choice," she said. "Just like us. We're always going to be a part of each other's lives, whether we like it or not."

That was true. But now I was beginning to think that having Mia in my life wasn't quite as bad as I originally thought it was.

"Careful. It's starting to sound like you like having me around." My left elbow leaned to balance my weight. "Are you—"

"Hell, no," Mia automatically said before I could even finish my question. "Not even if I needed a kidney and you were the only person available."

"Ouch. Don't take your time to think about it or anything."

Shrugging, she smiled so wide that her eyes squeezed into cheerful creases. Two dimples popped up on either side of her cheeks. I smiled back even though she had basically just insulted me.

But before I could say anything else, Mia grabbed my arm and pointed up at the sky. "Wait, is that one? It is, isn't it?"

"Uh . . ." I peered in the direction that she was pointing. There were some stray clouds, but I could make out a small light making its way across the night sky. Slowly. Way too slow to be a meteor. "I think that's just a plane."

"It is?"

Looking down at her hopeful face and pouting lower lip, I felt myself melting a bit. Didn't want to rain on her parade. "No, you're right. It definitely was a meteor." I lied again for the second time that night even though I knew that it was just a plane. "Better make a wish now before it's too late."

Her eyes lit up and she closed them. Hands clasped together in front of her chest.

I clasped my hands together, too, but didn't close my eyes. Instead I just looked at her. Watched her. In a totally non-stalkerish way. Being by her side was comfortable. Made me relaxed and happy.

A wide smile crossed her face as she opened her eyes, making me freeze. I couldn't do more than stare at the way the smile made her face brighten. At the way the moonlight hit her face perfectly, illuminating her features.

"That's one thing I can finally check off. I guess we could go to sleep now."

"Right." I was reluctant to move, but I couldn't think of a reason to stay.

I don't know if Mia was in a rush, but she climbed down the stairs right after me. Her legs were right above my face and her ass was coming toward me, molded in the soft cotton shorts Mom bought her for Christmas last year.

Shit. Shit. Shit. I gulped and looked away, but my mouth and throat were as dry as sandpaper by now. And my arms no longer knew how to function. I froze, but she kept coming down until my arms encircled her legs and now her butt was . . .

Yeah, this was a big mistake.

She twisted in my arms. "What's the hold up?"

"What? Sorry, there was . . . a bee in my face or something." I coughed and willed my arms and legs to move, but they wouldn't budge. They just clung on to the metal ladder like useless barnacles.

"Jake?"

I gripped the metal bars and twisted my head back to look up at her. At the same time, she leaned backward a bit so she would be looking directly down at me. Suddenly, I kinda wished I was a little taller. That I could climb up, touch her soft cheek, and kiss her.

DAMN.

I snapped back to reality. What the hell was wrong with me? I couldn't be thinking about Mia this way. Shouldn't be. But once the image of kissing her popped in my head, I couldn't get it out. And I had to physically force myself to pull away from the tiny house. Away from Mia. We needed to get out of here before I ended up doing something that would get my ass kicked.

Not even caring how far I was from the ground by now, I let go of the rungs and jumped.

There was a soft *thud* as she hopped to the ground right beside me. I don't know if she jumped down too quickly or if her feet were angled the wrong way, but her legs buckled and she swayed. I instinctively reached out and grabbed her. My hands wrapped tightly around her narrow shoulders.

"Thanks. That was weird. I got dizzy for a second." She held on to the side of my shirt to balance herself and peered up at my face. Her face was inches away from mine. I could see the faint smear of freckles across her cheeks. Just a couple. She used to complain about it all the time when we were kids, especially because no one else we knew had any.

Mia licked her lips, and my grip on her shoulders automatically tightened. Her hand lingered on my side, fingers pressing lightly against my back. A small breeze wafted past me, smelling vaguely of barbecue smoke and daisies. Who could still be barbecuing this late at night?

My brain yelled at me to let go of Mia before I looked crazy, but I didn't want to. Even though my nerves were on fire, I'd never been so comfortable or relaxed in my life. I just wanted to keep holding her like this forever. I liked holding her.

That bit of information hit me so hard that I automatically let go of Mia and actually backed up a few steps. It knocked the breath out of me as if I had just been tackled by the football team.

"Ah, shit."

Mia stopped dusting off her shorts and gave me a funny look. "What?"

"Oh, ah, nothing." I coughed and nervously scratched the back of my head. I didn't mean to say that out loud. "I was just saying it would suck if your wish doesn't come true. You know, shit."

That was the saddest recovery ever. I could tell by the look on her face that Mia didn't believe me at all. Instead of calling me out on it, she crossed her arms. "You know, if you really are worried about my wish coming true, then you should pick up the next time Finn calls."

"Why would you . . ." My voice trailed off, and I stared at her in amazement. "That's what you wished for? All those years searching for a meteor, and that's what you waste it on?"

Instead of answering me, she just tucked a strand of hair behind her ear and smiled. A sweet, happy smile that hit me like a bolt of lightning. "Good night, Jake."

MIA

BY THE TIME JAKE went home, it was already after 1 a.m. Mom was still asleep so I just crept into my room and got into bed. I tried to go to sleep, but my conversation with Jake kept replaying in my head. Or rather what he didn't say. The look on his face when I asked him about Finn. The hesitation in his answers. The sadness in his eyes.

He may not have said he wanted to see Finn again, but I could tell that he did. I knew that he did.

Making up my mind, I grabbed my laptop from the floor. Sliding in between my sheets, I opened my laptop and pulled up the unfinished email I had written that afternoon.

Hi, Finn,

It's been a while! I know you're probably surprised to hear from me. Especially since we haven't spoken in over two years since you left. I saw your emails on Jake's laptop so I just thought I would email you directly to say . . . How are you?

Okay, that's not exactly what I wanted to say. But really, how are you? How are things on the cruise ship? Is it all shiny and luxurious? Do you see dolphins and whales all the time? I bet you're even more tan and gorgeous than before. ☺

Mom and I are doing great. We still live across the street from Jake and your mom and we still go out to eat dim sum every Sunday at Royal House. They renovated last year so it's bigger now. More space between the tables so the carts don't knock your elbow quite as much. Definitely enough space for a fifth person if you ever decide to come back to visit . . .

Since we're on the subject, are you ever planning to come back? Mrs. Adler misses you like crazy and although Jake doesn't ever say it, I know he does, too. He's stubborn, but that just shows that he cares. For example, he doesn't respond or read any of your emails, but he still kept every single one. That's something, isn't it?

Just think about visiting before it's too late.

—Mia

And that was it. Short and brief. Well, okay, I kind of rambled a bit, but I basically said what I needed to say.

Before I lost my nerve, I hit the Send button and shut my laptop with a sigh. That was it. No turning back. Now I just had to see if and when Finn responded. And then . . . well, I didn't really know what would happen next.

Either way, Jake was either going to thank me or hate me, but at least I tried my best. Someone had to.

I WAS SO OCCUPIED with emailing Finn that I forgot about my lab report until the next morning. Not wanting to get a zero and risk Mom's wrath, I skipped breakfast to finish it. By lunchtime, I was torn between either starvation or risking my life by eating the brownish gray blob on my plate. The school claimed it was a "burger," but I'm fairly sure I saw something exactly like this on the chapter about fungus in biology a couple of months ago.

Maybe I could just eat the shredded cheese on top. Out of everything on the plate, that looked the least questionable. Which wasn't saying much.

I was poking at the cheese when someone bopped me on the head with a folder. "Why are you staring at your lunch like you're expecting it to pounce?"

"I wouldn't mind if it did. At least then I would know it's still fresh." My head turned just as Jake straddled the seat beside me. His arms clenched the back of the chair as he leaned toward me. My eyes zipped toward the brown bag in his hand. "What is that?"

"Oh, this?" He dangled it in front of my face like a pendulum clock. "Just my egg sandwich that I was going to toss out. Ms. Saunders didn't show up to fourth period so the class just hung out and ordered pizza."

Not sure if I was getting weak from hunger, I could feel myself swaying with the bag. "Lucky. What is this? The sixth time she didn't show up?"

"Yeah, I doubt she's going to have a job by the time she finishes planning her wedding."

"People do crazy things for love. So about that sandwich . . ."

He blinked at me and shook the bag. "What? Do you want it?"

"Uh, do you not see this drool?"

"Here." Finally! My hand grabbed at the bag, but he held it out of my reach. "If you promise to do all the dishes by yourself the next time Mom and I come over for dinner."

I grimaced. "Even the pans?"

"Everything."

I chewed on my lower lip as I considered his offer. Mom had a habit of cooking these huge feasts whenever the Adlers came over, and she somehow always ended up using every single utensil and plate in the kitchen. Which made doing the dishes a pain in the ass. Plus, she didn't like to use the dish-washer for anything but a drying rack, so washing everything took ages.

The image of the mountain of dishes flashed in my mind, and I crossed my arms. "Nope. Not worth it."

Just then, my stomach let out a big rumble. Seriously, the people at the table next to us actually turned to stare. Like they've never heard someone's stomach talk before. Or a bear growl.

Grrr...

"Well, then at least promise that you'll never call me a dork again," Jake bargained with a grin. His voice grew louder like he was a game-show host. "That's it. Just one tiny, measly, little promise for this deliciously fresh egg sandwich from Chef Adler."

"You're so lame. Fine, I promise..." I swallowed and tried again, but it was like the words kept getting stuck in my throat. "I promise never..."

The annoying smirk on his face widened. "Never...?"

Gah, the ass. He really was milking this for all it was worth. My jaw tightened, and I lifted my chin. "Forget it. A measly egg sandwich isn't enough for me to throw away my dignity."

"What if I tossed in a Twinkie?"

Now that's a game changer.

I eyed him. "You don't have one."

"You're right. I don't have one. I have two." He slid the clear package across the table at me like a peace offering. "I'll even give you the first one for free."

Damn, Jake wasn't playing fair. He knew all my weaknesses. And Twinkies were at the top of my vices. I've loved the sweet spongy delicious cake and creamy filling for as long as I could remember. Had to have at least one every other day. And that was because I gave myself a limit.

When Hostess stopped making Twinkies years ago, I went into a withdrawal. Like a serious withdrawal. It was a depressing and dark time. Especially because I had also hit puberty that same year so my hormones were already going crazy. Thankfully, Twinkies made a comeback less than a year later. I like to think that my Kickstarter campaign made a difference even though we didn't raise any money. Awareness still counts.

But I was stronger than this. I mean, women fought against discrimination to no end. They didn't give in.

Even as I continued giving myself a mental lecture, my hand reached out to grab the Twinkie, as if it had a mind of its own. Before I knew it, the creamy soft cake was in my mouth. And it tasted a thousand times better than usual. Probably because I was starving.

Okay, I was pretty ashamed, but it was kind of hard to hate myself when I was so happy. The sugar. The cream. Ah, this must be what blissful heaven felt like.

"So I actually had a reason for looking for you, and it isn't just to coerce you into doing what I wanted. Although it's pretty fun." He laced his fingers together on his lap. "I wanted to check if you needed a ride home today."

I licked the cream from my fingers, drifting back to reality. "Oh. No, I'm going over to Aly's house to work on our English paper."

Was that disappointment that flickered across his face? It disappeared before I could be sure.

Jake shifted back and forth in his seat. "That's cool. I figured I might as well ask."

"Okay. Thanks."

I expected him to leave, but he just sat there rocking back and forth like he was waiting for something. And I swear, with each rock, the chair slid a tiny bit closer to me. A millimeter. A centimeter? Were those the same? I sucked at the metric system.

"You know, you haven't called me Brat in a while," I blurted out instead.

"I guess I haven't." He pursed his lips a bit and my eyes zoomed down to them. "Why? Do you miss it?"

Jerking my gaze away, a slight flush crept down my face. I tried to be discreet as I fanned myself with my folder. "No, I just noticed it."

Jake's face grew thoughtful as he chewed on his thumbnail. "You're just less bratty these days. You're . . . something else."

My head cocked to the right as I peered over at him. "What am I?"

His eyes searched mine for a while before crinkling at the edges in an unspoken smile. "I haven't quite figured it out yet, but I'll let you know when I do."

That was barely a compliment, but at least it definitely wasn't an insult, so I didn't give my usual snarky response. "Have you decided if you're going to perform at the festival or not?"

Jake choked on the water he had just taken a gulp of. "What are you ... how did you know about that?"

"I have my ways." I handed him a couple of tissues from my bag. "Okay, Rose told me. Why are you ashamed?"

"I'm not *ashamed*." He ran his fingers through his dark curls, tugging at the ends a bit. "I just ... I'm not going to do it, that's all. So why bother telling anyone about it."

"That's just stupid. Not you." I stopped and thought about it. "Well, kind of you."

His brow rose. "Ouch."

Not wanting to start another fight when we just made up, I rushed to explain myself. "I don't mean it in a *bad* way. It just doesn't make sense to me. You have talent, and they want you to perform. This should be your dream come true."

"How do you know what I want?"

I scoffed. "Come on. Performing live in front of people has

always been your dream. Why else would you make me sit through so many of your 'concerts' when we were kids?"

"To torture you?"

"Well, it worked." There was a drop of water clinging—glinting—on his jaw, and I wiped it away so it would stop distracting me. There was the slightest bit of dark scruff on his chin that was rough against my finger. Jake stared at my hand, and I dropped it on my lap with a thud. "Seriously, forget everything else. Forget Finn and your YouTube channel. Forget the past couple of years. It's just you and the festival. What do you want to do?"

He shook his head. Hard, like he was trying to clear it. "I don't know. It's not that simple."

I let out a heavy sigh. Maybe it was still too soon for him. "And it's not that complicated, either. If it were me and I had a chance to perform onstage, nothing would stop me. Not even if a thousand Ryan Reynoldses were in my way. Or Ryan Goslings. No Ryan could stop me." Although I wouldn't mind if they tried . . .

"Then why don't you?"

"Why don't I what?"

The smile on his face twitched. "Perform onstage."

"Because it's pretty hard to get the part when you're talentless." I let out a hollow laugh. "It's okay. I've come to terms with it. I'm just not an onstage kind of person. That's for people like Lyndon and Ben. I'm just a backstage office person."

"Are you?" Before I could respond, Jake leaned forward, resting his jaw on his palm right in front of my face. "I still think you can be onstage. I wasn't lying about that. Seriously, you can do whatever you want. Don't underestimate yourself. You're amazing."

My eyes narrowed as I scrutinized his face, but he wasn't joking. If he were, then his left eyebrow would be arched a bit higher than the right. But the only thing I could see on his face was honesty. Pure honesty with no strings attached. And it hit me like a jab in the gut. Jake really did believe I could.

Mom said I was crazy with the whole theater thing, and to be honest, I'm pretty sure that's what Aly thought, too. But she was too sweet and loyal to say it to my face. Even I had a hard time convincing myself. Ben was super sweet and supportive, but I could see the doubt in his face whenever we practiced.

This was the first time that anyone told me that I could do this. And really meant it. Plus, it was amazing that this encouragement was coming from Jake. He knew firsthand exactly how bad I was.

"I know I'm amazing." I tossed my hair over my shoulder with a sigh. "But thank you."

Jake scoffed, but I could see a smile playing on his lips. "No problem."

"But you're not bad, either. Not as awesome as me, but still not bad," I admitted. "You should give the festival a chance."

His mouth opened and closed like he wanted to say something, but then he shook his head instead. "Tell you what. I'll promise not to waste my talent if you promise not to give up."

"Deal." I held out my hand. "Regular handshake or pinkie swear?"

He rolled his eyes. "What are we, ten?"

I gave him a bright smile and wiggled my pinkie at him. "Sometimes it feels like we still are."

"Things sure were simpler then."

When he hooked his pinkie against mine, I couldn't help remembering all the times we had done this when we were kids. All the promises and secrets. Then it all went away.

We haven't been friends for nearly ten years, but today it felt like we never stopped. And I was glad some things never changed.

JAKE

WITH A DISGUSTED SCOFF, Greg tossed his controller on the bed. "Okay, that's the third time I kicked your ass today. What's wrong with you?"

I dropped the controller at my feet and rubbed at my forehead. "Nothing. I'm just off my game. That's all."

"No kidding. It's so easy to beat you today that there's no point in playing anymore." Greg downed the last of his soda and crushed the can in his hands. "Seriously, your scores haven't been this bad since we switched from playing the Xbox to the PS4. What's wrong?"

"Nothing. I'm just not feeling it today." I leaned my back against my chair and kicked at the controller on the floor.

Just then, Rose snorted from her spot on the bed. I eyed her. "What?"

"Nothing. I'm just surprised that you guys are able to function for so long when you're so oblivious to everything."

Greg groaned. "Jeez, sis, you're grumpy these days. Did you date someone secretly and get dumped or something? It's not our fault if you did."

Her eyes didn't even lift from her phone. "Everything is your fault. You're my brother. But fine, if Jake wants to continue being in denial about being in love, then so be it."

I choked on the Coke that I had been drinking. It went straight up my nose and burned as I struggled to clear my airway. "What do you—I'm not—"

"Please, like that isn't a love song on your desk."

Greg and I both turned to look at the desk and lunged at the same time, but he was quicker. The sheets literally slipped through my fingers and even gave me a paper cut. Damn.

His eyes scanned the paper, getting wider and wider by the second until he resembled an anime character. "Whoa, I thought you didn't do the music thing anymore? What's all this?"

I jammed my cut finger into my mouth and shrugged, trying to look nonchalant as I edged a bit closer to him. "Nothing. I was just bored so I was fooling around. That's all. It doesn't mean anything." Just another foot. "And it definitely doesn't mean that I'm in love."

"I don't know, man. It sounds pretty lovey-dovey to me."

My face got red.

I couldn't concentrate on my classes all day—although I

doubt anyone could get through Mrs. Collins's lecture on the different points of limits. I swear, a part of me dies every time I step into calculus.

It started off as doodling, but before I knew it, lyrics came pouring out of me. Even faster than I could write them. Greg was right when he said that I hadn't written anything new in ages. Didn't feel the need to. I thought that part of me was gone. But this was different.

I was actually working on it before Rose and Greg came over and must have forgotten to put it away.

"Wait, how did you even know about this song?" Greg suddenly asked, turning to his sister.

"Please, like you two could ever hide anything from me. I'm a snoop," she said blankly without a hint of shame. "I know everything."

Greg scoffed. "Not everything."

"The second bottom drawer of the left side of your desk is fake." She paused and cocked her head to the right. "Actually, all three of the drawers on that side have a false bottom, but the second one is the most important one."

I turned to Greg. "What's in your second drawer?"

His ears turned a bright red. "No—nothing. There's nothing there. You know Rose. She's crazy. Especially in the beginning of the week. All that coffee," he rambled, glancing around the room like an escaped convict, tossing the sheets at me. "I forgot I have to go home and do something for my mom. Like right now." Greg glared at Rose as he backed out of the room. "And you can find your own ride home."

After he stomped down the stairs, I glanced over at Rose. "Do you want me to drive you home?"

"Nah, Greg will drive me."

"But he just said . . ."

With a smirk, Rose whipped a ring of keys out of her pocket. The Slytherin key chain I got her from Harry Potter World two years ago dangled on the end. "He's not the brightest crayon in the box, but luckily for him, he's blood so I'm forced to love him."

I shook my head. "I should send my condolences to Greg for having a sister like you."

"You should be glad you're an only child." Her face paled. "I didn't mean . . . I know Finn is . . ."

"I know what you meant."

"I should go before Greg bursts an artery or something. If you really work hard, then you could probably have that song ready for the festival," she called out over her shoulder.

"I never said I was . . . never mind." She was barely listening to me anyway. She and Greg were already arguing as they thundered down the stairs.

Appearing at my doorway a few minutes later, Mom shook her head in disbelief. "Seriously, those two are so loud, I don't know how their parents can stand it."

"Well, Mrs. Bell probably gets a discount on Advil at Costco so they're fine. They'll probably throw a party when they finally get rid of them after graduation, though." Grabbing my keys from the nightstand, I shoved my feet in the loafers by my bed. "Are you ready to go?"

"Not yet. I still need to shower, but I'll meet you downstairs in fifteen minutes?"

"Deal."

On the third Saturday of each month, Mom and I would go out on a "date." Not a creepy kind of date. Just hanging out outside the house. Sometimes dinner or a movie. Or both. We started the tradition after Finn left. Mom was mopey every day so I took her out. Even bought her flowers and chocolate, although Mia always ended up eating all the chocolate a few days later. And it cheered Mom up, so we went out again a few weeks later and the tradition stuck.

I didn't mind, though. It made me happy to treat Mom every once in a while. Make her feel special. Greg called me a momma's boy, but I didn't think it was necessarily a bad thing. That was the only reason I didn't kick his ass. That and the fact that Rose would have kicked *my* ass afterward.

After we got our first plate of food at China Wall Buffet, Mom grabbed a fork and wiped it down with her napkin like Mrs. Le taught us ages ago. Just in case. "So I'm supposed to ask you about some music festival again? Rose mentioned it to me before they left."

With a sigh, I shoved a couple of french fries in my mouth. "To be honest, I'm having second thoughts about it."

Mom's fork tapped on the side of her plate in a steady rhythm. "What's there to think about? That's awesome. You should definitely give it a shot."

"I don't know. I'm still debating—"

"Which means you've been obsessing about it for weeks." She laughed and shook her head. "You think I don't know you? I've been taking care of you since you were two. You overthink everything in life. Sometimes you just need to go for it. Do what you want. Without agonizing about the consequences."

I picked up my pizza and put it down again without taking a bite. "But I wasn't planning to pursue music again, so what's the point of starting all this up?"

"Yeah . . . about that." Mom folded her arms on the tabletop. "I think you should give that a shot, too. Like your brother."

For a minute or two, all I could do was stare wordlessly at her. "What are you talking about? Are you telling me that you want me to leave, too?"

"No! God, no. I love having you with me. But—"

"But?"

She reached out to pat my arm. "But I don't want you to be stuck with *me*. I don't want to be your prison. If you want to pursue music, then sing. Start by singing at the festival! If you want to travel the world on a cruise ship, then do it. Hell, if your dream is to become a dog walker, then I'll support you in that, too. Just do whatever *you* want." Her hand tightened. "Even if it means I'm not there. That's what your parents would have wanted."

I know her words were meant to encourage me, but they just weighed heavier on my heart. "But how could I do that when you've given up so much for us? I can't just ditch you."

"Well, I still expect you home for the holidays and dim sum Sundays once in a while," she said with a mock frown. "But let's face it. We can't live like this forever. Someday, you're going to get a job. Get married. Have kids. And our house isn't big enough for that. Plus, I'll be too old to take care of kids by then."

A wry laugh escaped my lips. "I thought your dream was for Mia and me to get married as soon as possible so you'd have grandkids to take care of."

With a smile, Mom played with her pasta noodles, pulling them from one edge of her plate to the next. "To be honest, it was hard after your uncle left. I know I wasn't the greatest mom—"

"You were the best mom."

She laughed. "You're sweet, but I was horrible. I burned your milk all the time and when you cried, I cried. If it weren't for Mrs. Le taking me under her wing and showing me how to be a mom, I don't know what I would have done. Then Finn left . . . it felt like our family was shrinking by the second. I think that's why I pushed you and Mia together all these years. I just wanted them to officially be our family. A complete family."

This was the first time Mom ever talked about Uncle Bran to me. I didn't know she felt this way, but I guess I should have realized it. To me, she was always there. Strong and unwavering.

"I'm so glad you two did get together, though. Although don't give me grandkids anytime soon. I'd like a couple more diaperless years first." She shoved her chair back and got up. "I need more sushi. Do you want anything?"

I glanced down at my still full plate. "No, I'm good."

After she left, I moved my sautéed green beans and pizza around on my plate. Ten minutes ago, I was starving, but now my appetite suddenly vanished. Instead my stomach was filled with knots and guilt as Mom's words filled my head.

Finally, Mom was giving me permission to do whatever I wanted. And how did I repay her? By lying to her face and taking away the only family she had left. This time next weekend, Mia and I would have our breakup and be out of each other's lives forever. Which meant the Les would pretty much be out of Mom's life, too.

I should be ecstatic, but I wasn't.

To be honest, I was already regretting this whole thing. Especially at the thought of never seeing Mia again. Never having her call me a nerd or having her sit in my car while she chattered on and on about everything. At first it had sounded amazing, but now it just made me more depressed the more I thought about it. Having to go on the cruise and see Finn wasn't nearly as important as keeping Mia in my life. I knew that now. I was pretty much ready to call the whole thing off the other day at lunch.

But then I realized that this wasn't just about me. It was also about Mia and what she wanted in her life. And she wanted me out of it so she could do whatever she wanted. Date whoever she wanted. I couldn't take that away from her.

I just didn't realize until now how much it was going to hurt Mom in the end.

But what else could I do? Either way, no matter what I did, someone was bound to get hurt. Mom or Mia. Mia or Mom.

And all because of me.

MIA

IF THERE WAS ONE thing I didn't mind about being stuck with the Adlers, it was that we always had company for dim sum. I mean, sure, Mom and I could always go by ourselves, but it's always better to go with a group. You can order a ton more stuff and not worry about having a mountain of leftovers for the week. That way, you'll be nice and refreshed for dim sum again when Sunday comes back around.

But as much as I wanted to focus on the soup dumplings and baked pork buns in front of us, Jake and I had work to do this Sunday. Because Mom had such a strong reaction to our PDA, we figured that would be a good way to make our moms realize that us being together might not be all cupcakes and rainbows.

I scooted so close to Jake that I was practically on his lap. But I had to be that close so he could wrap an arm around my shoulders. Mom and Mrs. Adler didn't seem to mind that much, but the little Chinese ladies pushing the carts kept giving us disapproving looks, so at least we were on the right track.

"Do you want another shu mai?" Jake asked, waving the little dumpling in front of my face.

My stomach churned in protest, but I forced a beaming smile on my face. "Of course, pumpkin. Although seven might be my limit. I don't want to have to roll out of here later."

He poked at my left cheek with a smirk. "I'll roll you around for the rest of my life if I have to because you're my boo boo."

Urgh. Now my stomach was really rolling. Maybe we were overdoing it with the pet names. Or maybe my stomach hurt because of the mountain of dumplings that Jake kept feeding me. Apparently, he thought the best way to show affection was to feed each other.

Mom and Mrs. Adler were eating it up, though. There were practically stars in their eyes while they watched us. This was their dream coming true right in front of their eyes. Their years and years of late-night scheming was finally worth it.

It almost made me feel bad about tricking them.

Almost.

Jake's hand tightened around mine as his thumb rubbed the sensitive skin on the inside of my wrist ever so slightly. Goose bumps ran up and down my arm, and I glanced over at him. He didn't even seem to notice what he was doing as he was eyeing the dessert cart that was rolling toward us.

Besides, our hands were partially covered by the teapot on the table so it's not like our moms could see. But if this wasn't for their benefit, then why was he doing this? And why the heck was it driving me crazy?

Maybe I was getting food drunk or something. Was that a thing? Or was it the allergy medicine I took this morning? Maybe that was making me woozy.

Yeah, that was probably it.

When I couldn't take it anymore, I jerked my hand away.

Jake glanced over at me, and I pointed at the sweet tofu soup, pretending that was the reason I pulled away. "Could I get a bowl?"

After she handed me a steaming hot bowl and stamped our card, the cart lady started to leave, but Jake held her back with a touch of his hand. "Could I get extra ginger syrup, too? With the ginger pieces?"

"Yes, yes."

To my surprise, he slid the extra bowl over to me. "What is this for?"

"You always complain when you're done that you wished you had extra ginger pieces to munch on to end the meal." He picked up his chopstick and grabbed some Peking duck and a bun.

Mom had a surprised look on her face. "Does she? I never noticed."

"Me neither." I scratched my neck, but I honestly didn't

remember ever saying that. Although it does really sound like me. "That's weird that you remembered."

His cheeks flushed a bit, and he shrugged. "It's no big deal."

"That's what happens when you're in love and don't realize it," Mrs. Adler cooed, grinning. "To be honest, I actually thought that you two might be lying about dating at first."

I choked on my soup and grabbed my napkin so I wouldn't spit soft tofu on everyone. With frantic glances over at me, Jake lowered his chopsticks. "What do you mean?"

"Well, it just seemed so abrupt. And, I don't know, weird? Like I couldn't put my finger on it. But now seeing you two together, it just warms my heart. It's so nice to be together like this."

"It's like we're one big happy family," Mom said as she patted Mrs. Adler's hand with a soft smile. "I hope every Sunday can be like this."

My smile was forced and hurt a bit. Especially because I realized that this was probably going to be our last dim sum double date with our moms. I mean, our two-week deadline was already half over. And surprisingly, the thought made me feel a little empty inside. Not that we wouldn't be pushed together anymore, thank God, but Mom was right. Jake and Mrs. Adler were practically our family. The Adlers had been around for as long as I could remember. And next week they would be gone. Who knows what we would be doing on Sundays from now on.

And Sundays were only the beginning. Vacations. Holidays. Dental appointments.

Okay, maybe I could deal with seeing the dentist on my own.

It's weird, but we had been so intent on getting our moms to get off our backs that I never really *thought* about what it actually meant. That we wouldn't be in each other's lives anymore. And we could do whatever we wanted from now on.

It was funny, though. Right now, I couldn't think of anything else I would rather be doing than eating dim sum with the Adlers.

AFTER WE GOT HOME, our moms went inside first so Jake and I could say goodbye privately. Although I'm not entirely sure how private it was because I was sure they were peeking out the windows at us. And probably with the phone in one hand and a glass of wine in the other hand.

We were both quiet for a few minutes now that we were finally alone. I leaned against the wooden fence that encircled my front lawn.

He kicked at a rock by our feet, and it clattered over to my shoe. "So what now?"

"What do you mean?"

"Our date is over. I guess we could either hug or—"

"Kiss?" Oh God, did that word come out of my mouth? My

face flushed, and I turned away to stare at the streetlight. "It's not like it's a big deal. We've kissed once before."

He let out a short laugh. "And I think we both agree that it wasn't that great. Or are you talking about the time when we were eight? Either way, it was not good."

With a scowl, I poked his shoulder. Hard. "Whatever, dude, I bet I could kiss circles around you."

Snorting, he grabbed my hand before I could try to poke him again. Instead of letting go, though, he brought it down to his side. "That's some confidence you have there."

My feet automatically took a step closer to him just as he took one toward me. Then another. Until finally, our arms ended up pressed against each other as we leaned against the fence. Side by side. From our shoulders to the back of our hands.

He leaned toward me for a bit and paused. "Are you sure about this? I mean, we don't have to actually kiss. We could make it look like we're kissing or—"

"We have to get the first kiss out of the way. Might as well do it now." Before he could say anything else, my other hand wrapped around the nape of his neck, and I tugged him down for a kiss. Nice and quick.

As soon as our lips touched, a jolt went through my body. It was like one of those cartoons when someone puts their finger in the socket. When the lightning zaps their entire body from their toes to the tips of their hair.

Letting go of my hand, Jake braced both hands against the fence behind me to kiss me harder. Longer. His entire body pressed against me so closely that my back was practically bent over on the fence. The only thought that flitted through my head was thank God for all those yoga classes Aly dragged me to all summer.

It was both weird and kind of comfortable at the same time. Our bodies knew each other. It was natural. The way my arms automatically wrapped around his waist and my palms pressed against his back, his shoulder blades. Melted into him. Our lips molded together. Over and over and over. It was almost like neither of us needed to stop and breathe.

Just when I thought it couldn't get any better, his left hand moved down my arm, lightly scorching a path as his fingertips caressed me from my elbow to my wrist. By now I had to literally hold on to his forearms so I wouldn't melt into the ground like an embarrassing Mia blob.

Where did these muscles come from? I saw Jake every single day, but I definitely didn't see these. Then again, I never held him tightly like this, either, so maybe they were always here and I just never noticed.

Jake pulled back slightly, and the cool air hit me in my face, bringing me back to reality. My head swirled like I had stood up too fast. What the heck just happened?

Breathing heavily to calm my racing heart, I gulped and my

hand tugged at the right strap of my dress, which had fallen off my shoulder. "So . . . yeah, I think that works."

"I guess so." He let out a slow deep breath, and it was like I could feel it.

We both stared at each other for a minute longer before jumping away from the fence. The last few minutes were weird. More than weird. That was crazy. Like something took over me.

I shook my head to snap myself out of it. His hazel eyes reflected the shock I felt, but when he bit his lower lip, I had the urge to kiss him again.

Seriously, what was wrong with me?!

"Mia?"

"Yeah?"

His face was turned upward as he stared at the stars. It was clear tonight. Barely any clouds in the sky, just twinkly stars against the midnight black sky. "Do you think maybe—never mind."

"What?"

"It's nothing. I forgot to tell you that you look really nice today."

Taken aback by his compliment—especially since I rarely ever got one from him—my cheeks automatically grew warm and I self-consciously brushed my bangs back out of my face. "Oh. Thanks."

"No problem." A small smile played on his lips. "Good night, Brat."

"Good night." The way he said "Brat" this time didn't sound like an insult anymore. It almost sounded . . . nice. Sweet. Like an endearment.

Oh God, what was wrong with me? This was *Jake*. He wasn't nice or sweet. Ever.

After Jake left, I came into the quiet house through the kitchen. Mom's light was off, but I swore it had been on as I walked up the walkway. I was glad she wasn't here, though. I was still confused about what just happened.

My cheeks were still flushed and warm, and I was nervous and anxious for some reason. My brain was yelling at me to snap out of my weird funk. But I couldn't do anything more than gulp down the water before pressing the cold wet glass against my forehead.

Ah, that felt good.

It took a little while for my head to clear. And even longer to make sense of what just happened. For a moment there, by the fence, we weren't Brat and Ass. We weren't forced to be together by our moms. We were just Jake and Mia. And to be honest, I actually *liked* having him around sometimes.

After I took a shower, I checked my email, but Finn hadn't emailed me back yet. Last time he responded within a couple of hours. Then again, the last email I sent him was pretty long.

To be honest, I felt guilty at first, but the more I talked to

Jake about Finn, the more I felt that he was ready to see Finn again. And he needed to move on.

Just as I jumped into bed, my phone beeped with a text message. Not remembering where I tossed my glasses, I squinted at the tiny bright screen.

> J. ASS: *Just wanted to let you know that those were some pretty big circles you ran around me tonight. I'm man enough to admit it.*
> J. ASS: *Don't let it get to your head.*
> J. ASS: *Good night.*

It took a couple seconds for his text message to sink in, but I had to bite the inside of my lip to stop myself from smiling when it did.

Oh, God, just the thought of that kiss made a rush of emotions flood through me. And the disturbing fact that I was feeling this way because of *Jake*.

Darn it. Darn it. Darn it. I should NOT be thinking about Jake. Not in that way. I tried to imagine Ben's face, but Jake kept popping back into my head with a stupid grin.

What I really needed to do was sleep. Obviously, I was overly tired so I was light-headed and delusional. That's it. Sleep. Once I got that then things would go back to normal.

This was going to be a long night.

MIA

AFTER REHEARSAL ENDED, I carried a couple of boxes filled with the musical programs across the room. Daniel, the theater director, cursed and hit the top of the table with his fist, which was still clenching his cell phone. "Stupid chemistry!"

I stopped. "What's wrong?"

"Dana Brennon just emailed me to let me know that she can't be in the musical anymore. Apparently, she's failing her chemistry class, so her mom grounded her until her grades come up." He scowled as he picked up a script and pen. "She could have come in and let me know in person. I don't know how we're going to find a replacement when the show is in less than a month."

"Her part isn't that big . . ."

"No, but Dana's part still has that solo in that one song. Not to mention, she's in the background for most of the scenes, so the person playing her still has to know what's going on." He shook his head. "I'll figure something out. Maybe I'll try to talk to Dana and her mom. Set Dana up with a tutor myself if I have to."

I was barely listening to Daniel. My insides were jumping up and down. I had been debating trying out for the next play or musical the theater did, but this was just too good to pass up.

Here goes nothing. With a deep breath for courage, I dropped the boxes on a nearby chair and tapped him on the shoulder. "Do you think maybe I could try out for Dana's part?"

Daniel turned to fully stare at me. "You . . . want to be . . . in the musical?"

I almost backtracked and said I was kidding, but Jake's face popped into my head like a mental cheerleader and I charged forward. "Well, yeah. It's actually always been a dream of mine to be in one. I mean, as much as I love typing out address labels, it's not exactly my top career choice." I tried to laugh it off, but it came out as a weak cough.

"Of course, I didn't think—" He broke off. "Do you think you can handle the part? I mean, the show is in three weeks. Have you ever been onstage before?"

"Well, no." My heart sank. Gah, I knew this was a stupid idea. "You're right. This is too important. I would probably screw it up. Forget I brought it up."

He reached out to grab my arm before I ran off. "Wait, I didn't mean—"

"I think it's a good idea," another voice called out.

We turned around and saw Lyndon standing a few feet away. Her stage makeup was still on, but she'd taken down her hair and changed into her regular clothes.

"It's a good idea," she repeated again. Probably because we were both still staring at her. At least I know that I was. "Mia's run lines with the other actresses a few times, and she's not too bad. Her singing could use some work. I've heard her singing to herself in the dressing room. Kind of off-key, but not horrible. I could work with her if you want."

I should have been offended and any other day I might have been, but I was still reeling over the fact that Lyndon said I wasn't "too bad." Actually, before today I didn't even think she knew my name, much less noticed me running lines.

Daniel clapped his hands together before nodding. "That settles it then. Why don't you see if you could get the costume from the back room for alterations, and we'll work out some extra time for you to practice and catch up?"

"Okay, thanks." I glanced over at Lyndon, who was already packing up her bag. "And thanks, Lyndon."

"Don't thank me. Thank him." She jabbed her thumb over her shoulder at Ben, who was beaming at both of us. "He wouldn't stop gushing every day about how great you are. I guess I'll see you at rehearsal tomorrow."

"Of course! I'll be here early." My voice was muffled as Ben grabbed me tightly for a hug.

"Congratulations! Guess you'll be onstage with me sooner than we thought. At least for the rehearsals. Should I get your autograph now while I still can?" He pretended to fumble as he searched his pockets for a pen.

I laughed. "I think we still have some time before that happens. But it's all thanks to you."

"You don't need to thank me." He cleared his throat. "Maybe you could go out with me this Friday night instead."

I blinked at him for a moment until his words sank in. "This Friday?"

"Yeah, I mean, unless you're busy . . ."

This was it. My dream guy was asking me out on the same day that I got a part in a musical. Two impossible things in one day. I should be jumping up and down for joy right now.

Just two weeks ago, I would have leaped at the chance to date Ben. It didn't matter that Mom would never allow me to. I would have found a way no matter what. But why couldn't I bring myself to say yes? And why did Jake's face keep popping into my head? And his kiss. At. This. Exact. Moment.

That kiss with Jake was throwing me off. Haunting me. And for no good reason. Sure, it was a good kiss. An amazingly damn good kiss. But it didn't actually *mean* anything. After all, we were doing all of this to get out of each other's lives. That's it. Nothing else.

And now I had a chance to go on a date with Ben. He was handsome and kind, and he helped me get a part in the musical. Even if he weren't my dream guy, I could still take him out to thank him. I'd be an idiot if I didn't. And I was definitely *not* an idiot.

I shoved all thoughts of Jake, that kiss, and everything else that was bothering me out of my head and smiled up at Ben. "I'd be glad to."

JAKE

MY PHONE BEEPED with a text while I was slicing the tomatoes at work. I glanced over to check it and couldn't help grinning at the goofy picture of Mia holding a bound book over her head like a heavyweight champ.

> MIA: *Get ready to see me onstage in a couple of weeks. I expect a bouquet of roses and a Twinkie to congratulate me.*
> MIA: *Kidding. Make it a box.*

I laughed at that, but I was glad for her. Maybe I should treat her to ice cream or something to celebrate later. At that parlor on Third Street. We hadn't gone there in a while, but they always had those weird flavors Mia loved to try, like goat cheese and mint with olive oil drizzle topping. Blah. Those things belonged on a salad. Not ice cream. Why eat that when you could get something that was actually good, like chocolate chip?

My phone buzzed again with a video from Mia. I clicked on it, and my smile faded when I saw Finn's face. Singing and grinning right into the camera. At me.

It was a recording that someone shot on one of the cruise ships. I don't know which one, and I have no clue how Mia even found this video. Finn was covering one of Adam Levine's songs. He'd been a Maroon Five fan since we were kids. He even loved the old songs that no one ever heard of.

He looked . . . happy. A part of me still resented the fact that he could be happy while he ditched Mom and me and made our lives hell for a while. But there was no denying that he looked happy. Content as he sang to the audience. He even did a little solo on the piano beside him. And the longer I watched him, the less I could stay angry. Especially at all the memories of him that came rushing back to me.

As I replayed the video, Mom's comments from the night before drifted through my head. And my promise to Mia. She looked so excited in that picture that it almost made me jealous. I couldn't even remember the last time I was that excited about anything. Maybe I should try to give music another shot. I mean, I didn't have to pack up and leave like Finn, but I could still do something. Anything.

I could even start off with that festival.

My thumb scrolled back and forth between the video of Finn singing and Mia's happy face before I made my decision.

> ME: *Hey, Rose, do you mind sending me the festival coordinator's number?*
> ROSE: *Nope, too late. I've badgered you for weeks. Now the window has closed.*
> ME: *Seriously?*
> ROSE: *Nah. I'll send you her contact right now. What made you change your mind?*
> ME: *I don't know. Just did.*
> ROSE: *Sure. Well, be sure to thank Mia when you make it big.*

Snorting, I started to type out a bunch of denials, but Rose's next words made me stop.

> ROSE: *She really is a good influence on you whether you admit it or not.*

I couldn't fight with that. She had a point. Mia had a way of making me do things I didn't want to do. Or at least I didn't even *know* I wanted to do it. If it wasn't for her, then I never would have even considered the festival. But now I was actually feeling excited.

Two weeks ago, I thought Mia was completely annoying, but actually we were just different. Very different. But maybe that wasn't such a bad thing. Tons of opposite things go perfectly together. Cold ice cream and hot fudge. Violins and rock music.

Different could be nice sometimes.

"HI, COULD I GET a turkey sandwich with extra meat, extra cheese, and all the toppings?"

At the familiar voice, I looked up from my cleaning and saw Mia grinning at me on the other side of the counter. I immediately smiled back at her. "What are you doing here?"

"Aly dropped me off on the way to the mall." She pulled herself upright to perch on the counter. "So, are you going to get me that sandwich or what?"

"How about you help me clean up so we can leave early?"

"Pass."

"What if I toss in a couple of free cookies?"

Her eyes lit up. "Chocolate chip or oatmeal?"

"Both."

"Well, what are we waiting for?" Mia grabbed the damp cloth from my hand and jumped off the counter.

Thankfully, there were a couple of cookies left over to bribe her with. Usually Rose worked with me and would take them home for Greg, but she had to switch her shift to take her dad on some errands. Some dinner they were planning to cook for their mom tonight. I didn't mind working alone. It was peaceful. Especially since there was a Texans game tonight, so we barely had any customers.

She wiped the glass cabinet beside the counter. I couldn't really tell because her face was downturned, but I could have sworn that she was blushing a bit. "So . . . Jake . . . I wanted to—" She broke off her sentence and chewed on her lower lip.

"Just spit it out."

Mia let out another deep breath. "I have a problem. I know this weekend we were supposed to have our big breakup, but I . . . have a date."

"Wait, what?"

"A date. You know, when two people go out to eat. Maybe catch a movie. Walk along the shore if we had one."

"A date," I repeated again, focusing on the most important word through all her rambling. "With . . . a guy?"

"No, with Dusty, the neighbor's dog." Mia let out an exasperated sigh. "Of course with a guy, you dummy."

I let the dummy comment slide. To be honest, it was still hard to wrap my head around the fact that Mia was *dating*. "No, I meant *what* guy?"

"Oh, just Ben—"

"Ben from the theater?"

Okay, now she was definitely blushing. Her cheeks were so red that she actually had to fan them with both hands. "Just forget about it. I'll figure something out myself."

We were both quiet for the next fifteen minutes, but I couldn't help sneaking glances over at Mia. She was busy refilling the straws and napkin dispensers, but I could tell that her mind was somewhere else. Especially with a faraway look on her face. She kept knocking over the box of straws and had to chase after them spilling across the tile floor. Probably daydreaming about her date with Ben already.

Finally, I came around the counter and squatted down next to her. I took the box from her hands. "If you want, we could delay our breakup. We could even double date with Aly so your mom won't suspect anything."

Her head lifted, and she stared at me. "You'd do that? For me?"

"You don't have to look so shocked. I can be nice sometimes." We were friends after all. Sort of. There was nothing wrong with helping each other out. To be honest, I wasn't *thrilled* about her dating, but I was actually okay with putting the breakup off a little bit longer. For Mia, of course. "I could use a free meal. I assume that he'll be paying for me, too, right?"

She tugged on a strand of dark hair, twisting it around her fingertips over and over. "I don't—if not then I guess I could—"

"I'm kidding." I shoved myself upright. "I'll just pick you and Aly up at your house, and we'll meet Theater Boy wherever you want. If you're really feeling appreciative, then you could offer to finish the dishes yourself. For the next ten years."

With a raised brow, Mia crumpled a napkin and threw it at my face. "Nice try. You're giving me a date, not your kidney."

"Hey, my weekends are very valuable." I caught the napkin with one hand and shrugged. "Still, can't blame a guy for trying. Ready to go?"

"Yeah."

After I set the alarm and locked up, I stepped outside where Mia was waiting for me by the steps. I dug my keys out of my pocket to unlock the car.

"Jake?"

"Hmm?"

She leaned back against the metal banister—hands gripping the rail—as she stood a step above me so our faces were almost level. She made a face before she finally got the words out. "Thank you."

Laughing, I leaned forward. My left hand was right next to her right hand. Our thumbs were almost touching. "You're welcome. Now, was that really that hard to say?"

She let out a deep breath and braced her hand against her heart. The spark was back in her eyes now. "Just never make me say it again. It left a nasty taste in my mouth."

I waved the bag of cookies in her face. "Don't worry. These will wash it out. Just do me a favor and don't eat in the car, okay?"

She laughed and grabbed the bag from my hand. Leaning forward, she gave me a quick kiss on the cheek. Barely an inch or two from my lips. "Careful, if you keep doing all this stuff for me, everyone's going to think that you actually like me or something." She flipped her hair over her shoulder. "'Course, how could you resist me?"

Mia was just joking, but the truth hit me like a mound of bricks. A punch to the gut.

To be honest, I didn't even notice her walk away and get into the car. Not until she honked on the horn to get my attention. I was too busy reeling from the earthshaking fact that she was right. I liked Mia. I *liked* her. No strings attached. No mothers involved. I just *liked* her. That's it. Always have.

And I just promised to help her date another guy.

Well, shit, now what?

MIA

"I'M EXCITED. IT'S BEEN a while since I've gone on an actual date." Aly's blue eyes sparkled as she dabbed a bit of perfume on her neck. "Even if it's totally fake."

"Uh-huh." Frowning, I attempted to curl the strand on the left side of my head. God, this sucked. My attempt to get that casual, tousled, all-I-did-was-brush-my-fingers-through-my-hair-but-doesn't-it-look-gorgeous hair was failing miserably. All I could manage was to curl my hair in stiff swirls around my head.

"It was nice of Jake to help you out."

"Yeah. He can be all right sometimes." Great, now my hair was frizzy from my frantic combing. I picked up the brush and pulled my hair into a high ponytail. There was no way I could save this mess. I applied a little bit of cherry lip gloss to my lips instead.

Grinning, Aly patted the top of my head. "I've never seen

you so frazzled about getting ready. You must really like Ben to be doing all of this."

I swatted her hand away. "I don't know what you're talking about."

My hand smoothed the nonexistent wrinkles on my jean skirt and flowy cream lace blouse. I didn't want to be over-dressed, so figured the skirt would be a good choice. Casual, sweet, but still gave Ben something to look at. Plus, I lotioned my legs like crazy so I knew they looked silky smooth.

To be honest, I wasn't *that* excited about the date. More nervous and apprehensive. But I figured at least I'd finally know what it would be like to actually go on a date with Ben. Plus, it actually helped my nerves a lot that Aly and Jake would be with me.

When Aly and I came downstairs, Jake was already wait-ing for us at the door. His hands were shoved into his khaki pockets as he kicked the ground with his left gray loafer. The nice canvas ones that he bought at the outlet in Houston. He must have bought four pairs of the same shoes in different colors that day. I thought he was crazy, but now I had to admit, they looked really good. Especially because he paired them with a blue collarless polo.

I was so busy looking at his outfit that I didn't notice it at first. But there it was. His quick glances in my direction as we all walked out to his car. Once. Twice. Plus, there was definitely a flicker of admiration that crossed his face. No matter how much he tried to hide it.

A warm feeling spread all over me, and I had to purse my lips together to hide my grin. Why did I care about what Jake thought about me? I never had before, but it felt nice to be admired. Even if it was just by Jake.

GOD, THIS WAS PROBABLY going down in history as the most awkward date ever. The definition of *Awkward Date*.

Well, the date started off fine. We met up with Ben in front of Tony's Slice to eat before the movie. And Ben was handsome and sweet. And taller than I remembered. Like he suddenly grew outside of school. Or maybe we had never stood this close together before.

Aly actually mouthed the word *Wow* and gave me a thumbs-up behind his back. And not very subtly, either. But Ben pretended not to notice.

Then it went downhill when we went inside and got our booth. Jake and I automatically slid in the left side together and grabbed the menus on the table. We didn't even realize anything was wrong until Aly cleared her throat and nodded at the right side of the booth.

Jake and I kind of froze for a second. Neither of us realized what we had done. It was kind of natural. Guess all those years of being forced to sit together finally paid off. Jake shot me an apologetic glance before climbing out so Ben could sit beside me.

When we were all in our correct seats, my stomach twisted in knots the closer Ben sat by me. My hand tapped on the edge of the table in an erratic pace until Jake nudged my foot under the table. Flushing, I grabbed my glass of water to take a sip just because I didn't know what to do with my hands. And then another one. And then another one. Before the waitress even read us the specials, I had already polished off my glass. Like I had just come back from a six-month trek in the desert or something. My mouth still felt dry, though.

Ben looked over at me and smiled. "Do you want more water? I could get you some."

He stood to head toward the drink station, but I grabbed his arm. "No, I'm good. But, hmm, thanks."

"Okay . . ." He sat back down, and this weird silence surrounded our table. Like tumbleweeds-rolling-in-the-desert type of silence.

It was so weird. Ben and I talked just fine during rehearsals. I mean, I was still a tiny bit nervous around him sometimes, but we were starting to get more comfortable. I didn't even plan out our conversations anymore.

I definitely wasn't a total wreck like I was now.

Maybe it was because we weren't at school in the theater anymore, but on an actual date now. But it was most likely the fact that whether we continued on as friends or became something more depended on this date.

So no pressure.

After our food came, Jake cleared his throat. "So where are you going to college, Ben?"

"I'm actually planning to take a break from school. Maybe continuing working at the theater. I feel like it's hard to convey realistic emotions onstage when you don't know anything about life." Ben smeared a bit of butter on a breadstick. "I might try out the whole college thing next year though."

"So basically you're just going to hang out for a while until you get bored and leave?" Jake coughed. "I mean, the theater."

"Well, I'll let Daniel know before I go anywhere." He glanced over at me and smiled. "Besides, I might decide to go to college here. There are a lot of things I like in this town. The people especially."

Did that mean what I thought it meant? I wasn't sure, but I couldn't help grinning at Ben like an idiot while he ate his slice of pizza. Maybe this date wasn't going as bad as I thought it was. Even though Jake was being pretty rude.

He was acting like my mom interrogating Ben or something. Even worse than Mom. And I'm pretty sure that if she wasn't so crazy about Jake, she would have jumped ship to Team Ben.

Jake speared a couple of slices of tomatoes from my salad

plate, and I slid the pepper over to his side. He shook it over his fries. "I think our parents would kill us if we tried to pull something like that after graduation."

"My parents are actually great. They want me to follow my dream..." Ben's eyebrow rose as he looked back and forth between our plates. "Why did you take her tomatoes?"

"Because Mia hates them. Always has." Jake waved his fork in my direction. "But her mom always made her eat them before she could leave the table so she'd pass them to me. Either that or no internet for a week."

I rolled my eyes. "You act like it wasn't a two-way street. Who ate your oatmeal for you every Saturday morning? Plus, whenever we go out, I always get a different dessert so we can share."

"Yeah, but that's still more for you than me. You're the one addicted to sugar."

"Fine, then how about—"

With a confused half smile, Ben waved a hand between us to get our attention. "Okay, but why are you eating her tomatoes *now*? Your parents aren't here. And why don't you just order the salad *without* the tomatoes if you don't like them?"

That shut us both up.

Huh. That never occurred to me before. To either of us. Like sitting on the same side. Jake ate my tomatoes. I ate his oatmeal. And we always sat next to each other. That's the way things always were. It never occurred to us to change it.

Ben looked a little sheepish. "I mean, there's nothing wrong with it. I just think it's kind of funny, that's all."

I laughed weakly. "Yeah, funny."

There was still another tomato slice on my plate, and it was like our eyes kept zooming to it like moths to a flame. But neither one of us moved. Finally, I covered my plate with my napkin. Jake turned away as I gulped at my water.

Even though Jake was just across the table, it felt like he was miles away.

JAKE

WE FINISHED DINNER EARLY, mainly because Mia and I didn't really feel like eating much after the whole tomato incident. That was the first time I'd ever seen Mia turn down dessert.

She was usually such a chatterbox. I mean, to be honest, getting her to be quiet was usually the problem. But she barely said a single word all night. The most she did was giggle and brush her hair over her shoulder. A lot. Except her hair was pulled up so she was really just tossing air over her shoulder, which pretty much made her look crazy.

All because of *Ben*.

God, I really hated that guy. From his polite smile to his shoes. Okay, I might have been a little biased. Especially because I wished that I was the one who was by her side. And he was nice. He actually paid for dinner even though I tried to pay half. Snuck and did it without any of us knowing. He wasn't a cheapskate.

He seemed pretty cool and all, but he just wasn't Mia's type. She needed someone who understood her. Who knew that something was up if she was quiet. And someone who knew how to make her happy.

Okay, *maybe* she looked pretty happy so far, but still.

"Do you want to go to the arcade?" I suggested when we got to the theater. "Since we're early. Movie won't start for another twenty minutes."

"Sounds like fun." Aly linked arms with Mia and tugged her ahead of us. Ben and I fell in step behind them.

The arcade entrance had all the action games that everyone usually crowded around. There was a group by the dancing game near the front. A group of jocks surrounded the basketball hoops and air-hockey table. Some smaller kids were playing Skee-Ball. One of the older ones was even cheating as he stood on the side and lobbed it into the fifty-point hole.

But down the hallway were the older games. Racing tracks, shooting games (deer and zombies), and Space Invaders. And in the far-right corner were the oldest—and coolest—video games. I mean, really ancient. Frogger. Asteroids. Donkey Kong (the original). All the classics.

"What do you guys want to play?" Ben asked, glancing around the arcade.

"Time Crisis 5," Mia and I both said at the same time.

"She spends more money on that game than she does on clothes," I explained with a snicker.

"Jake doesn't bother playing that game with me because he knows how awesome I am."

"She's a beast." No use denying it. There was a tinge of pride in my voice, but I couldn't help it. I was proud of her skills. And if we ever went to war or were under attack, then I wanted Mia on my side.

Unfortunately, there were a bunch of kids crowding around the game. We had to settle for some air hockey instead. I picked up the black puck and tossed it into the air at Ben. "What do you say? First one to seven points?"

He caught it with one hand and grinned. "Sure."

It was hard to keep the smirk off my face. Especially when Mia threw me a warning look. I gave her an innocent one in return. Don't know what she was so worried about. We were just two guys playing an innocent game. And if I happened to wipe the floor with him, then so be it.

There was just one thing I didn't count on. Ben was good at air hockey. He was really good. And in no time, he was kicking my ass.

The puck slid into my goal, and I cursed.

"Six to two," Aly called out. She gave me a sympathetic smile. "Game point."

Mia peered over at me with a wrinkled brow. Her face was like the emoticon with question marks around its head. My face flushed with embarrassment, but I refused to look away. It took every ounce of willpower and pride—what little I had left—to meet her gaze.

A slight sparkle was back in her eye as she pushed past me toward the Time Crisis game. "Actually, I want to play Time Crisis before the movie starts. Ben, want to be my partner?"

"Uh, okay."

There was still one kid playing, but one look at the fierce expression on Mia's face and he accidentally let himself get shot. After that, he ran off so quickly, it was as if he teleported.

At first, I was worried that she was going to go easy on Ben. Let him get all the points. But her competitive side overrode whatever feelings she had for the guy. Before long, she was her old self again as she played, getting through each level with ease.

Mia was so focused that she didn't even notice that Ben stopped playing to watch her. Her eyes were glued to the screen, and she gripped the plastic gun and shot with such accuracy that I would be pretty worried if we weren't in the arcade. Her foot tapped on the pedal to duck every time someone popped out, barely a second before she would have gotten shot.

You know, I'd never admit this out loud and especially not

to Mia, but there was something really hot about a girl playing video games. Forget the high heels and push-up bras. *This* was what guys really wanted.

"Come on, Mia!" As she neared her high score, I got so excited that I put both hands on her shoulders, massaging them before the next mission started. They were both tense at first, but as soon as I touched her, she seemed to relax and soften. My thumbs rubbed against the tender spot beneath the nape of her neck and unintentionally touched her warm skin above the neckline of her shirt.

Mia glanced over her shoulder at me. Her eyes were wide and a bit startled. She wasn't the only one. I was surprised by how the unintentional caress made me feel. My hand tingled like a bolt of lightning hit it, but I didn't pull away. Time almost felt like it stopped and everything else faded away.

We've seen each other practically every single day for a majority of our lives. The day we learned to talk and the first day of high school. I couldn't pinpoint exactly when she became pretty. But I knew that this was the moment where she became more than just pretty. She was beautiful.

Bang!

We both jumped at the loud sound. A terrorist shot her screen, ending her game. "Damn it."

Not noticing the moment—or whatever the hell that was—between us, Ben leaned onto the machine with a grin. "That was pretty cool. Jeez, I didn't know you were a master at this game."

She giggled again, and I forced myself not to gag from the cheesiness. I couldn't tell if he was being sleazy or if he was genuinely this lame. The girls seemed to be eating it up, though. If this were an anime, there would be stars coming out of both Mia's and Aly's eyes.

As they walked away, Ben reached out and took Mia's hand, lacing her fingers through his for a few seconds before placing it on his arm. She looked at him in surprise but didn't pull away. The uneasiness in my stomach came back.

No, I wasn't biased. I just *didn't* like the guy. At all. And I didn't like the fact that it should be me beside her, holding her hand and smiling down at her.

Instead, all I could do was stand in the background and watch as the girl I liked walked away with another guy.

MIA

ALY SKIPPED AHEAD OF US with a happy bounce in her step. "That movie was so cool! I didn't expect that surprise ending at all. 'Course, I guess that's why it's called a surprise. We definitely have to watch it again."

Ben laughed. "I guess we'll have something to do next weekend. Are you in, Mia?"

I was so lost in thought that I barely heard their conversation. It wasn't until Jake snapped his fingers in my face that I realized they were all looking at me expectantly. "What? No, I'm not hungry."

Jake gave me a funny look. "That's good because nobody was offering you food. We were just talking about the movie."

"Oh, yeah, I thought the movie was . . ." I hesitated and stared at each of their faces for a minute before guessing. "Good?"

Thankfully, I guessed right by the nods and smiles on Ben's

and Aly's faces. Thank God for fifty-fifty chances. Jake was still eyeing me, but I avoided his gaze.

To be honest, I wouldn't have been able to tell anyone what the movie was about if they paid me. I was so nervous sitting next to Ben that it took every ounce of willpower I had to stop my leg from bouncing. Aware of every time he moved his hand and every breath he took. Not to mention, I could barely concentrate with Jake burning holes into the side of my head with his stares the entire time.

A part of me actually wished that this date wasn't happening. Then I could just hold on to the dream of Ben falling head over heels for me because the *actual* process of doing that was so much harder than I thought.

But the other part of me was just yelling at that part to stop being such a wuss and enjoy myself before the night was over. Or before it was midnight and I had to go home before my carriage turned back into a pumpkin as my fairy tale disappeared.

"It's still a little early. Do you want to get some ice cream?" Ben asked, piercing my daydream.

Jake's mouth opened, but Aly grabbed his arm and tugged him toward her before he could say anything. "You two go ahead. We'll just head home first. I'm kind of tired." Her left hand rubbed at her temple. "You don't mind, right?"

"Uh, sure," Jake said, his eyes still on me.

"Are you okay?" She had crazy piercing migraines sometimes. Even had to stay home from school a few times before. Maybe one was creeping up now. "We could—"

"No, go ahead. I'm fine." Aly pushed both of us along and gave me a wink behind Ben's back. Her eyes were bright and not at all in pain. "You two just go without us."

Oh. OH.

"Well . . . do you want to head out, then?" Ben asked.

"Sure." My eyes kept peering behind me at Aly and Jake. Especially at her arm looped through Jake's. She gave me a thumbs-up, and Jake still looked a little uncertain. Probably mirroring the look on my face, but he gave me a small wave as we walked away.

After Ben and I stopped by the ice cream shop, we decided to walk in the park a bit. There were a couple of people still around. Families with small kids on the playground. A couple sitting beneath a tree who looked like they were trying to eat each other's faces.

"So, what's with you and Jake?"

I nearly spat out my vanilla ice cream with olive oil drizzle (don't knock it until you've tried it) in Ben's face. He must have noticed because he dodged to the left, out of the line of fire. "What do you mean?"

"I mean, have you two ever . . ." Straightening, Ben moved his two fingers in circles. "You two seem pretty close."

It took me a moment to get his drift. "No, nothing like that.

I told you that we grew up together and our moms really want us to date, but we never did."

"Until now."

"Now is just to get them off our backs. It's not real." Is it just me or did my voice sound sort of wistful?

Stepping around a puddle on the sidewalk, Ben laughed. "I was just asking. I mean, I don't want to step on any toes if you guys are actually dating or anything."

"No, there are no toes anywhere." The meaning of his words sank in, and I looked up at him. "So, hypothetically speaking, if there were toes, you would actually be worried?"

"Realistically speaking, yeah." With a slow grin that made my toes curl against my sandals, Ben carefully took my half-eaten ice cream cone from my hand and tossed it into the metal trash can at the corner of the sidewalk.

He leaned over and kissed me gently. Sweetly. He brushed a wisp of my hair behind my ear while his hand was pressed against the brick wall over my head, making me feel small and dainty. But he left enough space between us so I didn't feel overwhelmed or crowded. My hand reached up to clasp the back of his neck and pull him closer.

Crazy as it was, the first thought that popped into my head as soon as our lips touched was that I wasn't done with the ice cream. Seriously, such a waste.

I mean, don't get me wrong. The kiss was ... nice. Really nice. Probably an eight on a scale of one to ten. Definitely top five of my favorite kisses. And this was dating back to my first kiss with Jake when we were eight and I kissed him as revenge for telling on me to my mom about my F on the earth-science project.

But I was still *disappointed*. I mean, I wasn't expecting a fairy-tale kiss that would sweep me off my feet or something, but I thought I would feel *something* more from my dream guy. I felt more electricity when Jake accidentally touched my neck. And not to mention Jake's kiss the other night. I mean, that went straight up to the top of my list. Now that was like a fairy-tale kiss. If fairy-tale kisses were rated PG-13.

Thinking about Jake while I was kissing Ben didn't feel right. It almost felt as if I were cheating, but on who? Jake was my fake boyfriend while this was my first (and maybe only) date with Ben. Technically, I was barely dating anyone, so it was kind of hard to be cheating.

That still didn't make me feel better.

Ben just smiled and took my hand to walk again. "Come on, I'll take you home."

Relieved that he wasn't going to try to kiss me again, I nodded.

AN HOUR LATER, I was still wide awake. I paced around my room, but I just couldn't sleep. There was a restless feeling in my arms and legs every time I tried to lie down. It just felt like there was something beneath my skin wanting to break free. Like an alien on the Syfy channel. I stretched. Wrote an email to Finn. Showered. I even tried to meditate, but nothing worked.

After my fourth attempt to do a cartwheel ended up with me in a crumpled heap on the floor by the window, I noticed that Jake's light was still on across the street. That was weird. It was almost two in the morning. What was he still doing up?

I grabbed my phone from my nightstand to text him.

> **ME:** *Are you sleeping?*
> **J. ASS:** *Zzzzz*
> **ME:** *I'll take that as a no. Especially because I can still see the lamp on in your room.*

His bedroom light immediately turned off and I snorted.

> **J. ASS:** *Perv.*
> **ME:** *It's only considered a perv if I'm leering at you & I can definitely assure you that I'm not. I'm just nosy.*
> **J. ASS:** *At least you admit it now.*
> **ME:** *And at least you admit that you're not sleeping.*
> **J. ASS:** *I never said that.*
> **ME:** *Well, you're still talking to me, aren't you?*

I could see that he was typing something, but he would keep erasing it and start over. Rolling over to my side, I propped my head up on my bent arm and waited for his response. It took a while, but finally he sent another text.

J. ASS: *Do you mind if I come over?*

My fingers paused on the phone screen. Now? It was practically two. Why would he want to come over?

ME: *Sure, meet me on the porch.*

Grabbing a cardigan, I tossed it over my tank top and shoved my feet into my ragged purple bedroom slippers. I couldn't help stopping to put some ChapStick on and comb my hair first, though. Just because I was rolling around all night didn't mean I needed to look like it.

When I got outside, Jake was already waiting for me on the porch. He sat on the top step with both hands clasped together over his knees. The hem of his navy sweatpants rose a bit, and I could see the Superman socks I got him last Christmas. The set of superhero socks were a gag gift, but the dude actually ended up loving them. Wore them practically every day. Even to church.

I sat down beside him. "So, what's going on?"

"Nothing. I just wanted to talk."

"Talk," I repeated, glancing around. "At two in the morning."

He ducked his head a bit and cleared his throat. "So, I've been thinking a lot about what you said, and I think you're right."

"I know. I'm always right," I automatically replied. "But refresh my memory on which time again? There are just so many."

He rolled his eyes. "I'm talking about the festival. The one and *only* time that you were right."

"Ah, that time." I paused. "Wait, so you're going to perform? Like in front of everybody?"

"In front of everybody."

I let out a high-pitched squeal that was so loud that I wouldn't be surprised if neighbors' windows vibrated. Jake rubbed his ears with his fingers, but he couldn't keep the proud dopey grin off of his face.

Then . . . well, I'm not exactly positive what happened next. One minute I was squealing and then the next second, my arms were wrapped around his neck in a hug. My butt was barely touching the porch as he hugged me so tightly that he lifted me up. "So, the festival. I'm going to perform one song on Friday night. Just to dip my toe back in and see if I even still like it. It's no big deal."

No big deal my butt.

"Stop being so modest. What are you going to sing? A cover song or do you have something new?"

He cleared his throat. "There *is* a new song I might want to try out, but I'm still thinking about it."

I poked his arm until he looked over at me. "I can't wait to hear it. And I'm proud of you. Seriously."

"Thanks." To my surprise, he reached out to tuck a strand of my hair behind my ear before kissing my cheek. Lightly. Like he was afraid I would break or run away.

But he didn't have to worry about that at all. Before he pulled away, I touched his right arm. Enough for him to pause and without a second thought, I went for it.

This time the kiss was softer than the one by the fence. Sweeter. But still as sweepingly overwhelming as the first kiss.

My fingers dug into his forearms—feeling his warm skin beneath his shirtsleeves—as I held on. His arms encircled my body and pressed against my shoulders as his hands stroked my neck. It was like he was everywhere. Like he didn't know where to stop. But the entire time his lips stayed firmly on mine as he kissed me. Over and over. The longer the kiss went on, the more I didn't want it to end.

Finally, reluctantly, I had to pull away to catch my breath. Jake stared at me, but he didn't move. His right hand was still pressed against my lower back, which tingled. "What was that for?"

"I . . ." I let out a deep breath to calm down, but it didn't seem to help at all. My heart was beating like a jackhammer.

Especially because he was so close, and all I wanted to do was kiss him again and again. "I don't know."

But I did.

There was a reason why I thought Ben's kiss was okay while Jake's kiss turned my world upside down. Why I wanted to sit next to Jake at dinner. Why I couldn't wait for my date with Ben to end, yet I jumped at the chance to meet Jake at two in the morning.

And the answer was simple. I liked Jake.

MIA

NOW THAT I KNEW I liked Jake, the last place I wanted to be was stuck in the car with him. It was awkward. So awkward that I half wanted to jump out the window to escape.

That was the only way I could describe the car ride with Jake. Actually, I could have used the words *uncomfortable*, *goose-bump-raising tension*, and *just plain weird*, too, but *awkward* pretty much summed it all up. Mainly because of the way I practically jumped his bones and then ran back into the house afterward.

Okay, to be honest, my stomach fluttered when he came to pick me up. It had been fluttering all morning. No matter how many chewable Tums I ate that morning. Plus, he looked kind of adorable in his best faded jeans and polo shirt. It was so crisp that you could almost see the iron lines on the shoulders.

I had come to terms with the fact that Jake was cute. The fact that I liked him was taking way longer.

Hating Jake was so much easier than liking him. Then again, maybe that was because I was starting to realize that I never really hated him in the first place. I was just too blind to see what was in front of me.

And if that was the case, then life just got so much more complicated.

I don't know why I didn't just cancel this car ride with Jake. I could have gone with Aly. She was free. But I had to lie and tell Jake that she wasn't. I just—I don't know—felt like going with Jake. Talking to him. Being with him.

Once we turned out of our neighborhood and got on the freeway, it was like all the words in the universe melted away. We gave each other brief smiles as the hum of his engine filled the car.

I fiddled with the air-conditioning in front of me, and Jake immediately turned it down. "Sorry, were you cold?"

"Uh, no, I was just playing with it."

"Oh."

It got quiet again except now it was even worse because there wasn't the soft hum of the AC anymore. God, this was the worst car ride ever.

When I finally couldn't take the silence anymore, I switched the radio on. Since it was still early, there were a bunch of people talking. I kept changing the station until I got one with some country music. Not my favorite, but way better than listening to people.

Jake waited until I got settled back into my seat before manually switching the station with the button on the steering wheel. At first, I thought it changed because of the car or something, but when I changed it back, he switched it as soon as I sat back.

His mouth twitched slightly as he stared at the road in front of us.

I glared at him. "Seriously?"

"What? I didn't do anything." His eyes widened. "Maybe it was a ghost."

"Don't use my worst fear against me." I poked his shoulder. "Just because that worked on me when I was eight doesn't mean it'll work on me now."

"Can't blame a guy for trying. Especially since you're just as naive now as you were back then."

"If by naive you mean brilliantly awesome, then yes. I guess I haven't changed."

Jake snorted and shook his head. "Nice to see you putting that dictionary I got you for Christmas to good use."

"Oh, definitely. It squishes the bugs in my room really well. Especially at night."

He smacked his forehead with his right palm. "Why do I bother arguing with you?"

"Because you have nothing better to do?" I twisted in my seat so I could fully face him. "Or because you secretly love me so much?"

"You wish."

Before I could say anything else, I spotted something fall out of the truck a few lanes over. The car beside us swerved into our lane to dodge it. "Look out!"

Jake slammed the brake. My body jerked forward from the sudden stop, and my hand smacked against the door. Luckily, he threw out his right arm to brace me even though I had my seat belt on. My shoulders hit his arm. Hard. And I flopped back into the seat.

Jake immediately pulled over to the side of the road and turned to me. His face twisted with anxiety. "I'm so sorry. I didn't see—are you okay?"

"It's okay. I didn't get hit or anything." I unbuckled my seat belt to stretch up and show him I was fine.

His eyes followed my hand and then lingered on my face before zooming back to the front. Jake rubbed the bottom of his jaw and neck. It was red and a little blotchy. He cleared his throat a couple of times. "Are you sure? What about your hand?"

Before I could respond, he reached out and picked up my hand, cradling it in both of his. His finger stroked every inch of my hand, examining it for God knows what. My breath got caught in my throat, but I didn't want him to let go.

And that was the exact reason I jerked my hand back. "See? I told you. Fine."

Instead of moving back, Jake leaned into me a bit. His face

dipped toward mine. Like he was going to kiss me. I held my breath but didn't move. But before his lips touched mine, he just tugged the seat belt against me. The click was abnormally loud. Then he zipped back to his seat like he was jerked back by an invisible string.

My heart was still slamming away so hard that I could hear it in my ears. Not sure if it was because of our near accident or Jake, I nodded. "What about you? Are you okay?"

He stared at me for a couple of seconds. "I'm good."

Something about the way he said that—so slow and soft—made me melt a bit.

God, it was hot in here. As he drove, I opened my window and stuck my head out a bit to cool my burning face. I didn't care if I looked like a crazy dog. The air in the car was so heavy that I could barely breathe with him next to me.

After taking in a few gulps of fresh air, I looked over and saw Jake practically doing the same. His left hand tapped at the bottom of the window, and his jawline and neck looked redder than before.

I knew why my heart was pounding a mile a minute, but why was his? "Are you sure you're okay? You look flushed. Maybe we should pull over or something. If you want, I could drive."

He laughed. "I'm fine. As long as you're in the car, things aren't going to change."

"Well, if you want me to leave—"

"That's the problem. I don't want you to leave." Finally, Jake looked over at me and held my gaze. "And if we pulled over right now, I don't know if I could stop myself from kissing you."

As the meaning of his words sank in, my eyes widened and all I could do was stare at him. He looked as shocked as I felt, and he abruptly turned back to the road and flicked the radio up loud. I swear, the windows were almost vibrating from the volume.

It didn't matter, though, because my head was swimming too much to hear the music. It was like all the new facts were bubbles dancing around my head, bumping into one another.

I liked Jake. And now I was *pretty* sure that Jake liked me. But I was sort of dating Ben. Plus, Jake and I still had to break up this weekend.

But one bubble grew and grew and popped all the other ones.

Maybe we didn't have to break up.

Maybe . . .

JAKE

CLEARING MY THROAT to get rid of my nerves, I tried to look cool as I sat down across from Mia in the cafeteria. She stopped doodling in her notebook and sat up straighter, probably looking as awkward as I felt. "What's up? Got more treats to bribe me with?"

I laughed. "No, I'm fresh out today. Unless you want me to pick something up after rehearsal today?"

She hesitated. "Actually, I don't have rehearsal today. We could . . . hang out. If you want."

The urge to fist pump was overwhelming, but that would probably defeat the purpose of acting cool. I couldn't help leaning closer to her, though. "Okay, then I'll just meet you in the parking lot after class. I wanted to talk to you about the festival—"

Just then, her phone rang on the table, bouncing against the surface and making us jump.

Mia fumbled with the phone before pressing it against her ear. "Hello? Oh, hi, Ben." My head snapped up, and she glanced over in my direction before lowering her voice. "No, I'm not doing anything right now."

I strained my ears to hear as I pretended to read the flyer on the wall about student council meetings.

"...this weekend..."

"Yeah, I don't..." She cleared her throat and shifted back and forth in her seat. "I'm still not sure. Can I call you back? My lunch break is almost over. Okay, bye."

A few minutes passed before I caved and finally spoke up. "So that was Ben?"

"Yeah, he was just calling to—he just called."

"Sounds like he was calling you for a date."

Her face got red. "A little bit."

I forced myself to plaster a big smile on my face. Especially when all I wanted to ask her was why she was still dating him and kissing me at the same time. What the hell? "Looks like he really likes you. If you need me to cover for you again, just say the word and Aly and I will be there. It was fun last time."

Before she could say anything, Aly plopped down on the seat beside Mia. "Hey, Jake! So did your moms rope you guys into going to school together again today?"

Mia's eyes widened, and I gave Aly a confused look. "What do you mean?"

"Well, I was going to drive Mia, but she texted me and told me that she had to go with you because of your moms—"

"Ha HA." Mia waved her hands between our faces, flapping like a bird. "You—you must have heard me wrong. I didn't . . . so, anyway, did you need something, Aly?"

Her face was still scrunched up. "Yeah, do you want to meet me by my locker or yours after class?"

"Why would we—" Mia's hand smacked her forehead. "Crap, I forgot about today."

"How could you forget the new K-drama with your future husband! We've been counting down for ages."

"Future husband?" I asked with a raised eyebrow.

Aly laughed and wrapped an arm around Mia's shoulders. "The gorgeous Lee Jong-suk. His new drama just came out, and it's deemed to be THE epic love story of the year. Like the price of tissues in Korea probably increases every Wednesday and Thursday night when it airs."

Mia gave me a sheepish smile. "We made plans ages ago to binge watch it once all the subtitles are up. So I guess I can't go home with you this afternoon. Unless you want to join us?"

A whole night of watching Mia drool over some movie star? I think I'll pass. "Uh, not at all, but thanks for the invite."

"Your loss." Aly grabbed a french fry from Mia's plate. "What were you guys talking about before I showed up?"

Mia and I exchanged looks. "We were just talking about the music festival this weekend that I'm performing at," I said.

"Both of you could come. *Should* come. I could use the support."

Aly's face brightened. "Cool, we'll definitely be there. Maybe Ben can come, too. And I'll spend the night at your house to 'console' you after your big breakup."

Mia's face dropped. "Oh, right."

"Aren't you excited? It's finally all going to be over."

Excited wasn't exactly the word I had in mind. More like dreading it.

And it was starting to feel like I wasn't the only one. I couldn't point out exactly what it was, but it felt like Mia was changing around me. Like she felt different about me. Or maybe we both were changing and realizing that we were in each other's lives for a reason. I know I was.

But the kisses. All the time we spent together. It had to mean something, right?

I tried to catch Mia's eye, to see if there was any chance, any doubt about the breakup, but she wouldn't meet my gaze.

Any hope I had deflated like a balloon that had just been untied. Guess that was my answer. I couldn't even make her look at me, much less pick me. Maybe it was all in my head after all.

JAKE

WITH A SIGH, I shifted my weight from side to side. "There will be food at the festival, Mom. You don't have to make me anything."

"You're already not letting me go, and now you're going to deny me the right to feed you, too?" She gave me a mock pained look as she piled a bunch of apples and blueberries into the blender. "Where did I go wrong as a mother?"

"I'm not trying to be ungrateful, but the smoothie and..." I picked up the plastic container and tried to peer inside. "What is this?"

"Just a simple chicken quinoa salad. I packed dressing and croutons on the side for you, too. And unsalted almonds for a snack."

Pressing a fist against my mouth, I had to struggle to swallow back my laughter at the earnest look on her face. "Quinoa...

Mom, the other musicians are going to laugh in my face if I bring these."

"Then you can just laugh in theirs when they get dehydrated and their voices crack from all the alcohol and fried food. Besides, almonds are a great source of protein and—" She turned the blender on, and the *whirring* drowned out all the other benefits to almonds. Maybe they could have made me grow six inches and fly. I guess I'll just never know.

Mom poured the weird concoction into a silver thermos. "Break a leg. I know you're going to be awesome."

"I'm pretty sure that's just an expression for the theater," I said, laughing as I grabbed the lunch bag on the table. Thank God, she packed my lunch in one of the navy-blue bags and not the flowery ones that she got off of the shopping channel last year. "But I'll try my best. Thanks, Mom."

"You can thank me when you win a Grammy someday." Just then, a car honked in the front, and she shoved me toward the door with a smirk. "Now go before Rose and Greg decide to come in here and get you. I don't need a headache tonight."

With a smirk, I pointed a finger at her. "Careful or I might ask them to sleep over tonight."

Her glare was fierce. "Do that and I'm going to the nearest hotel."

——————

I WAS SURPRISED THAT everyone was already in the Bells' van when it pulled into my driveway. I was even more annoyed to see Mia and Ben sitting in the middle seat together. All cozy. With Ben and his stupid smiling face.

Gritting my teeth, I fought the urge to scoot in between them. Instead, I sat in the back with Rose. With her knees propped up on the seat in front of her, she balanced her tablet on her lap while she worked on some video. I couldn't really see anything on the screen with the glare coming through the window on her side.

Mia turned and grinned widely at the lunch bag on my lap. "Did your mom leave a good-luck note for you in there, too?"

"Ha, very funny." Actually, that sounded exactly like something Mom would do, so I didn't check. "But there's a quinoa salad in here with your name on it."

"Yeah, I think I'll pass." She turned to nudge Ben's shoulder. "You didn't get a chance to eat lunch, though, right?"

"No, and I love quinoa." He gave her a big dopey grin that she returned.

I fought the urge to roll my eyes. Seriously, this dude. Who the hell actually *likes* quinoa? The only reason *I* ate it was because Mom made it so often. She claimed it was the next new superfood or something.

Still, I handed over the lunch bag so I wouldn't look like a complete jackass. I half considered just eating it myself, but I didn't know if I could keep it down. My stomach had been in knots all day. Plus, I was barely able to sleep at all last night.

Around eleven or so, it finally sank in that I was about to make my comeback . . . in front of hundreds of people. And this would be my first time performing without Finn.

I always wondered if he missed me when he left. Or was nervous about performing on the cruise ship alone. Probably not. Finn was always the stronger one. He didn't fall apart when our parents died. Even though I was only two, Mom said I cried at night for weeks. He wasn't anything but calm and reassuring until the day he left.

My leg bounced so much that Rose elbowed me. Hard. Pretty sure I'd have a bruise on my side. I stopped, but that didn't make my nerves go away. I tried to concentrate on something else. Anything else.

Suddenly, a pack of sugar-free gum landed on my lap. Surprised, I looked up and Mia gave me a half smile. "I don't want to be dragged to the dentist office for the next few months just because you ground all your teeth down to stubs."

I popped a piece into my mouth. "Thanks."

She glanced over at Ben, who was on the phone, before turning her entire body to face me. The side of her face pressed against the headrest. "You don't have to worry, you know. You'll do fine."

"Who said I was worried?"

"Just saying."

Man, I never could hide anything from Mia. I reached out and tucked a strand of hair behind her ear. "Thanks though. For the gum and . . . other things."

Instead of jerking away like she always did, Mia reached up to grab my hand and squeezed it with both of her own. "No problem. That's what I'm here for."

The longer she held my hand, the more I could feel my nervousness start to fade away. Like her confidence in me was transferring from her body into mine. It was amazing. And I didn't want to let go. Not even when Rose started clearing her throat. If anything, it made me hold on tighter so Mia wouldn't pull away.

Just then, I noticed a small thin band on Mia's finger. It was a spray-on gold ring with a heart-shaped plastic gem in the center. I hadn't seen it in over ten years. "Is this—where did you find this?"

Mia looked surprised as she pulled back her hand. "I found it the other night under my nightstand when I was cleaning my room—"

I held up a hand to stop her. "Wait, hold the phone, you were *cleaning* your room?"

She rolled her eyes. "Fine, I only did it because I spilled a plate of Cheetos on the floor. Happy?"

"That's more like it. Continue."

"That's it. I found it under my nightstand." Her fingers

rubbed at the surface of the fake heart gem. "It was wedged between the leg of the bed and the nightstand actually. I'm kind of surprised that you even remember it."

Ben hung up his phone and leaned back toward us. "Remember what?"

Mia turned to answer him while I glared at the side of his face for butting into our conversation. "This ring. Jake won it at the arcade ages ago when we were kids, and he gave it to me as a birthday present."

"Really?" Rose finally put her tablet away and peered over the rim of her glasses to squint at the ring. "It's kind of cheap. . . ."

"Initially, he tried to win the remote-control car, but he kind of sucked at all the games. This was all he could get," Mia whispered loudly with a snort.

"Excuse me, this is the thanks I get for giving up my winnings to buy your present?" I said. "And to think you cried for a week straight when you thought you lost it. We were worried that your eyes were going to be permanently swollen shut."

"What? It was the first present I ever got from a boy. And even though it was just from you, it's still special."

"Just from me?"

Blushing, she waved her hand. "Well, you know what I mean."

Mia didn't know it, but she was wrong. I wasn't trying to win the remote-control car. I deliberately lost so I would have the chance to get the ring for her. This was when we were still friends and not bothered by our moms' matchmaking. When things were simpler.

A sudden thought hit me. "You know what? Let me borrow the ring."

"Why?"

"You were lucky enough to find such a priceless gift after all this time. Maybe it might give me luck for the performance later."

"That sounds kind of crazy. And you hate all of that super-stitious stuff." But even as she complained, she slipped off the ring and handed it over. "Just remember to give it back later."

The ring was still warm from her hand. I put it over my left pinkie, and it fit snuggly over the second knuckle. "I know because it's special. Even if it was just from me."

Mia gave me the tiniest little grin, but her eyes sparkled with amusement. I couldn't help smiling back. "Yeah, just you."

Rose poked her head up, interrupting our moment. "Maybe you can just keep this ring and get Mia a new one if every-thing works out. One that's not so lame."

"Jake isn't lame. He's sweet." Mia suddenly glanced over at Ben and coughed. "I mean, the ring—giving it to me is sweet."

Smirking at Rose, I leaned back in my seat with the ring firmly on my hand. Mia turned back around, but I could see her looking at me through the reflection on the window. Our gazes met and I grinned. Her eyes widened, and she immediately turned away.

Whistling under my breath, I turned to look out my own window. Suddenly, I wasn't nervous about the festival anymore because I wasn't alone after all. I had Mia on my side and that was enough.

MIA

ONCE WE WERE INSIDE the front gate, we separated. Rose and Greg followed Jake to the backstage while Ben got the food. Aly and I were on drink duty. There was already a long line that wound down the sidewalk. Thank God I had a bottle of water in my bag.

Twenty minutes later, the bottle was empty, but we finally made it to the front of the line. After she placed our orders at the drink tent, Aly turned to me with crossed arms. "The tension in the van was really weird. I wanted to jump out of the car to escape."

I grabbed a bunch of napkins and stuffed them into my pocket. "Was it? I didn't notice."

"Are you kidding me? It was like the last season of *Game of Thrones* in there." At my blank look, she clarified, "It was cold. Because winter is here."

With a snort, I rolled my eyes. "Don't exaggerate. Jake was probably nervous about performing. That's it."

She pointed a finger straight at my face. So close that her nail nearly touched my nose. "Aha! If you didn't notice anything, then how did you know I was talking about Jake?"

The guy pouring the drinks in the tent snorted.

"Excuse me, if I wanted a side of snooping with my Coke, then I would have ordered it." I gave him an icy glare before tugging Aly to one of the freestanding tables on the side.

She tossed a curious glance over her shoulder at the guy before turning to me. "Seriously, what's going on between you and Jake? Are you friends? Dating? Or is he still your mortal enemy?"

What were we?

I took the longest sip of my life—nearly emptying the red plastic cup—so I wouldn't have to answer right away. Because I *couldn't* answer right away. I didn't know what we were. Just a few weeks ago, I shuddered every time I heard our names together. But now it was different. I still wasn't sure exactly when I started liking him. And why. He was still Jake, and I was still Mia. Yet we weren't.

But it's not like we could just start dating. I didn't even know how he felt about me. I mean, one minute he was talking about wanting to kiss me, and the next he was offering to set up another double date with Ben.

I used to be an expert at knowing exactly what Jake was thinking. That the wrinkle above his left eyebrow meant that he was amused and when there was a deep one that slashed across his forehead that meant he was pissed. How he tapped his left foot against the ground if he was forced to sit still for too long. But now . . .

It was . . . complicated.

God, that sounded cheesy. Like I was one of those girls online who wanted to make her relationship status seem mysterious, but there was no other way for me to describe it.

Gah, I needed an aspirin. All this thinking was giving me a headache.

"I don't know what we are." I jabbed my straw at the half-melted ice, swirling it around.

"And don't forget, you still have Ben." Aly let out a deep sigh. "Here you are with two guys, and I'm all alone. When did I become the funny single friend in your drama?"

Noticing the slightly downcast look on her face, I tossed the empty cup into the trash a couple of feet away. It bounced on the rim twice before falling in. "You're not just the single friend. And the only reason you don't have a boyfriend is because all guys are idiots. Who needs them anyway? All they're good for is reaching for stuff on the top shelf and eating all of your leftovers."

The corner of her lip jerked into a reluctant half smile. "At least I still have you."

"And you always will." Balancing the tray of drinks in one hand, I looped my other arm through hers. "Come on, let's get a good spot before the evening performance starts."

She laughed, but her arm tightened around mine and we maneuvered our way toward the stage. Even though it was still a little early, there was barely any space to walk between all the lawn chairs and beach blankets that were spread out. It helped that the weather was pretty awesome this year. Last year was so muddy that people had to throw away their shoes afterward. Instagram was full of pictures of barefoot people walking to their cars.

Luckily, we were able to grab a spot right by an oak tree for some shade, just managing to spread our own blanket out between a group of middle school girls and an older couple making out. Like seriously older. Probably about Mom's age. People around us gave them funny looks, but I didn't mind the PDA.

Then again, if it were my mom, then I'd probably be gouging my eyes out with my own fingers.

". . . and let's get ready for a brand-new artist. Although some of you might know him from the YouTube channel The Adler Brothers." The announcer—Ashley or Ashlee, the way she stretched out her name until it sounded like five syllables—said with a laugh as she tossed her perfectly blond hair over her shoulder. "Let's give it up for Jake Adler!"

My hands cupped over my mouth, and I cheered when

Jake came out. He hesitated for a second or two on the edge of the stage until Ashley/Ashlee waved him out. Finally, she had to loop her arms through his and pull him out. Although she still didn't let go when they got to the center of the stage.

"I heard that you're debuting a new song tonight. Is it for your girlfriend?"

With a shaky laugh, Jake glanced out at the crowd. "No, not a girlfriend. Not exactly."

"Not exactly? And what *exactly* does that mean?"

I leaned forward on my hands as I waited for his answer.

He dragged his fingers through his hair, tugging a bit at the end. His cheeks and forehead were a bit pink. "Uh, it just means that I don't have a girlfriend."

"Interesting. I guess this means that we'll just have to find out more later." She winked at the crowd. "Now, let's give it up for Jake Adler, you guys!"

When Ashley/Ashlee bounded off the stage, Jake let out a deep stammering breath and gripped the microphone with both hands so tightly that I could practically see his fingers turn white. The little gold ring on his pinkie glinted in the light. "This is my first time performing in front of such a large crowd. Or in front of any crowd actually. Let's just say that you're a lot more intimidating than the camera in my bedroom."

A few people laughed at his joke.

"Obviously, stand-up comedy isn't my thing." More laughter this time. "So let's just cut to the chase and get to the singing, shall we? I hope you enjoy."

I couldn't help feeling like a proud mama as I watched Jake up there. Sure, he was a little clumsy and nervous at first, but all of that seemed to melt away with each word that he sang. There were no ifs, ands, or buts about it. He was meant to be up there. He was meant to be doing *this*. I was so happy to see him up there that my cheeks ached from my huge grin.

Aly nudged me with her elbow. "I forgot how good Jake is."

"He is pretty amazing." I shot her a side-glance. "Don't tell him I said that, though."

"'Course not. Can't let him know how you really feel about him."

Greg popped up between our shoulders like a freaking jack-in-the-box. His bright blue sunglasses perched crookedly on the top of his head as he turned his head to look at me. "Exactly how *do* you feel about our Jakey boy, here?"

Without looking over at him, my index finger pressed against the center of his forehead until he was off of my shoulder. "I feel like Jake should be a little pickier about his friends from now on."

"Ouch." His hand pounded at his chest. "That really hurts."

Aly snorted. "Does it?"

"No. I'm pretty much used to rejection by now. No matter how harsh. Just bounces right off."

"Must be a talent of yours." I patted his shoulder with a grin. "Your only talent."

"Double ouch. And the hits just keep coming." He shook his head as he moved away.

Aly shook her head with a laugh. "Oh, well, at least he's nice to look at."

I glanced over my shoulder at Greg. "I guess so. Not really my type, though."

She gave a meaningful nod toward Ben, who was sitting behind us with Rose. "And what exactly is your type? Or should I even bother asking?"

Instead of answering her, I just shrugged and turned back to watch Jake onstage. He cradled the microphone with both hands as he moved around on the stage, stopping to wave at a little girl near the front. She hopped up and down with excitement.

The song wasn't that long, but it almost felt as if it went on forever as I continued to listen to Jake sing, as if time slowed down. Or maybe I just didn't want him to stop. With each word, each lyric he sang, this weird tingling feeling swept over me like I was in a trance. And I swear, even though we were too far back for him to see me, it felt like Jake was singing straight at me. To me.

Which was crazy. I mean, the festival was pretty much packed. The entire lawn was filled with so many people that we probably looked like colorful blobs to Jake. Like ants at a picnic. If ants wore crop tops and strappy wedges. There was no way that he could know where we were. It would have been easier to find Waldo.

But I still couldn't brush the feeling off. Especially when he sang about finding a love who was always there. Right next to you your entire life. And the moment you finally opened your eyes and saw them bright and shining in front of you. A part of you.

Each sentence hit me like a bolt of lightning. This was more than just a song sung to me. This was exactly how I felt. I needed Jake in my life. I wanted him there. And it was obvious now that Jake felt the same way.

JAKE

WITH A LOUD WHOOP, Rose raised her cup. "To Jake. Hopefully when he wins his Grammy, he'll say my name first in the list of people to thank."

"Why should he? I'm his best friend," Greg complained as he downed his drink. "*Best* friend."

"Sure, you keep telling yourself that." She patted the top of his head, squishing the dark spikes that he probably had spent ages on.

He let out a yelp and ducked out of her reach behind Aly, even though she was so tiny that she barely covered him at all. His hands gripped her shoulders, and she giggled so hard that she snorted into her Sprite. The camera on the second floor by the DJ zoomed in on them for a few seconds, showing them shoving each other back and forth on all the TVs surrounding the bar before showing other people in the crowd. The festival coordinators booked the entire bar down the street for the after-party, so we didn't have to worry about being underage.

"Don't worry, neither of you will be number one. That honor would go to my mom." I paused. "Then I'd thank Mia."

"Me?" Her eyes were wide with shock as she stared at me. "Why?"

"Because you convinced me to give all of this another chance," I said. Usually, I would never compliment Mia, but it was true and I was going to give credit where it was due. "So thanks."

With a soft smile, she tossed her hair over her left shoulder and clinked the tip of her glass against mine. "No problem."

Rose wiggled her left eyebrow knowingly at me before holding up her glass. "Then here's to Mia."

"To Mia," everyone else echoed.

After she finished her drink, Mia slipped off of her stool and slung her purse over her shoulder. "In that case, I think I'll get the next round. Could you help me, Jake?"

"Sure."

Luckily we had left the festival a bit early so we were able to snag a table in the corner, but now the bar was starting to fill up. My hand automatically pressed against Mia's lower back as we wove our way through the crowd toward the drink station. Her shirt was soft and thin. I could feel the warmth of her skin beneath my fingertips.

Wait—No, was that—

I looked down to be sure. The edge of her shirt had ridden up, and my hand was touching her bare skin. Just a tiny bit of it. And now I couldn't look away. Especially because I just noticed that my hand was right above her butt. How did she put on jeans that were so tight? It was like this pair was molded on. How did she even breathe?

"So I've been wondering something. . . ."

My head snapped up. I felt like the word *perv* was probably plastered all over my face. "Yeah?"

Thank God she didn't seem to notice. "Your new song is great. I mean, I'm kind of surprised you wrote it. Since it's about being in love and stuff. 'Course, you probably just wrote what sounded good."

"Well, I . . ." My mind raced to figure out the right answer. One that wouldn't scare her off. Because the truth was enough to scare me.

But even so, I was dying to tell her the truth. That it was all about her. That each emotion and thought while I wrote the song was all about her. That I was falling in love with her.

Before I could answer, some drunk dude in a leather jacket who was holding a can of beer stumbled toward us. Next thing we knew, the foam shot out and sprayed toward both of us like a sprinkler.

Shit. I grabbed Mia to pull her out of the way, but it was too late. My back and half of her shirt and hair were drenched. She gasped and blinked rapidly in shock.

"Look, man, I'm sorry. I don't know what happened. The can just leaped out of my hand or something, I swear ..."

With a fierce scowl, I held the guy back when he tried to wipe off Mia. More to protect him than her. Her nose flared up and that usually meant she was going to explode any second. And I sure didn't want to end this night with a bar fight. "Just go. And next time watch where you're aiming that thing."

With widespread hands, he had just faded into the crowd when Mia snapped back to her senses. Her wet hair whipped in my face as she spun around. "That jerk—where did I—I'm going to kick his ass."

Wrapping an arm around her shoulders so she couldn't run off, I tugged her toward the corner. "Just forget about it. He probably won't remember anything you say anyway."

"Still ... God, my hair's already starting to feel all sticky and gross." She picked at my wet shirt and grimaced. "You must be dying right now."

I was. It was as if I could feel every single drop on my neck and back. But I was more concerned about Mia. Particularly how her shirt was now sticking to her chest like glue.

Grabbing a couple of napkins from the bar, I dabbed at her hair and neck. "We're going to have to get you cleaned up before we go home. If you go home smelling like beer, then your mom will kill me."

The left corner of her mouth quirked up into a half smile.

"If she does, then it sure would have saved us a lot of trouble these past few weeks."

I rubbed at the spot above her ear and drifted down to her cheek. She cocked her head slightly to the right to give me better access. "I don't know. Were the past couple of weeks that bad?"

"I guess it could have been worse." She reached up and swept my hair off of my forehead. Her fingers gently ruffled through my hair, tugging a bit at the ends. Each of her movements sent a wave of awareness through my body. Of how close we were. How I could just dip my head and kiss her within seconds.

It took every ounce of willpower I had to pull away from her before I did something crazy. Tugging the little ring off of my pinkie, I handed it to her. "I should give this back before I lose it. Guess this was pretty lucky after all."

Mia laughed and slipped it on her finger. It fit perfectly. "Then it's a good thing I found it. Don't worry, I'll let you borrow it from time to time. At a reasonably low price."

I echoed her laugh, except mine was nervous and overly loud. "I have a confession to make. You know, back then I wasn't really trying to get the remote-control car. I wanted to get the ring. For you."

"For me? Why?"

This was it. Now or never. I let out a deep breath. "Because I liked you."

Silence. The bar was still loud, but I knew Mia heard me by the way her dark eyes blinked rapidly as she gaped at me. "Wait, you what?"

Now that I finally said those three little words that I had been dying to say for ages, it was like a huge weight had been lifted from my shoulders. "I liked you back then. A lot actually. But we were just friends so I didn't think I should say anything. I didn't want to ruin our friendship. And then we *weren't* friends anymore so there was no point in saying anything."

She tugged on her earlobe and laughed. "That's so weird, because I liked you back then, too."

Now it was my turn to stare at her. "Uh, what?"

Her cheeks were tinted pink, and she turned toward the bar, away from me. "Yeah, you were, like, my first crush. For a while actually. But like you said, things happened. We grew up. And now we hate each other."

Dropping the crumpled napkin, I slid between Mia and the bar to cup her face with my hand. Gently. Softly like she would break. Which was silly because she was one of the strongest people I knew. Kryptonite would melt in her presence. "I don't know about you, but I'm definitely not feeling any hate right now."

"Then what are you feeling?"

It felt like her question was physically between us, hovering in the air, separating us.

And I pushed it aside and took a step toward her. I didn't say anything. Mia looked startled at my closeness. Her eyes widened, and she stared at me. Then they flickered down to my mouth. Once. Twice. She pursed her lips. Damn. Now I couldn't look away from her lips. They were so soft and sweet looking. Almost shiny, but not in that fake glossy way. Just . . . perfect. It was like she understood exactly what I was thinking. Her face softened and before I knew it, she was in my arms.

Did she come toward me or did I pull her to me? I wasn't sure, but honestly, I didn't care. All I knew was that she was right where I wanted her to be. Snuggly and perfectly in my arms.

Nothing else mattered.

MIA

I KNEW WHAT WOULD HAPPEN if I went with Jake to get the sodas. When we were alone. What would happen if I stayed here any longer. If I leaned in. But I couldn't make myself move. Another part of me had taken over. The dumb, irrational side that if I could, I would drag home to kick her butt later.

His eyes were like two magnets reeling me in closer and closer until we were barely inches apart. His left arm was braced on the wall over my head, enveloping me into a cocoon. A Jake cocoon. I closed my eyes to try and control myself, but it didn't help. His breath was warm against my cheek. My fingers reached out to push him away, but I could barely do more than curl my hands around his forearms. We were so close yet still not close enough.

Everything and everyone else faded away, and the only

thing that mattered was his warm skin pressed against my arm. There was something almost desperate about his kiss. Like he had been holding back for so long. Or maybe it was me projecting my feelings on him. All I wanted to do was get closer to him, even though we were practically melted together. My fingers gripped his neck, and he held on to my waist with one arm as the other caressed my back. Lightly, like he was afraid that I would disappear. Or—

There was suddenly a loud cheer and uproar that dragged us back to reality.

Still in a daze, I glanced up and barely registered that everyone was staring at us. Cheering like we were some kind of celebrity couple.

Whoosh! My breath came out so suddenly that I felt like I was about to collapse. I almost wished that I did. Melt right into the ground and disappear. Especially when the crowd parted a little bit and all of our friends stood in front of us. I froze with Jake's arms still wrapped around me. Greg was so gleeful that he was practically jumping up and down. Aly looked amused. And Ben . . . Ben's face was hard like I had never seen him.

Behind everyone, I could see our picture on the large TV screen as though we were on some kind of hidden-camera show.

With a smug smile, Rose crossed her arms. "Looks like you guys decided to do a bit of celebrating without us."

"Not that we mind. Celebrate as much as you want." Greg waved his hands at us. "It's a free country. If you want, we'll—"

My face was flaming with each word Greg said. Luckily, Jake punched his shoulder—hard—and got him to stop talking. Greg groaned and doubled over in pain. I didn't have time to worry about him, though. I was more concerned about Ben. Especially when he just turned to Aly, whispered something in her ear, and walked away without a single glance in my direction.

The smile faded from Rose's face, and she cleared her throat. "Why don't we head home? I got all the footage I need, and I don't have much time to work on it tonight."

"Yes," Aly and I both said at the same time.

Jake glanced over at me but didn't say anything as he fell into step beside me.

We all shuffled out of the bar after Rose like we were being punished. A couple of guys patted Jake on the back with wide grins, but he just kept turning around to look at me. His forehead wrinkled with concern.

Ben was standing outside by the parking lot staring at his phone. When he saw us, his face scrunched up. He shoved the phone in his pocket and crossed his arms. "I called an Uber, but it's still ten minutes away."

"Why don't you go home—"

"No, I'm good," Ben interrupted, still not looking me in the eyes. "I can wait."

My mouth opened, but I didn't know what to say. What could I say? Sorry? Somehow, I didn't think that would be enough.

I was so wrapped up in Jake and me that I completely forgot what this meant for Ben and how he felt. I mean, technically, we were sort of dating. I knew he liked me. More than I liked him, and I kissed Jake anyway. Twice. Once in front of everybody.

Gah, I was horrible person. I wouldn't even date me if I could.

Luckily, Aly always knew what I was thinking without having to be told. She stepped up between us—blocking my view of Ben—and touched his arm. "We can't leave you here. Just come home with us. You can sit in the front with Rose. I'll sit in the back . . . with everyone else."

After a minute or two, he nodded. I let out a silent sigh of relief.

If Aly thought the car ride to the festival was awkward, it was nothing compared to the car ride home. Rose turned up the radio full blast, but the tension was swirling in the air around us. And even though we were barely an hour away from home, it felt SO. Much. Farther. Not to mention, we must have caught every single red light on the way.

I sat in the middle row with Aly, but I could see Ben's reflection staring out the window in front of me. Every once in a while, Aly would pat my hand reassuringly. I didn't even dare turn around to look at Jake.

Oh, God. This was probably what hell was like. Forget fiery pits, this was the worst torture of all. But I gritted my teeth and counted down the minutes until we got home.

Once we got to my house, Aly and I slid out at the same time. Jake got out, too, and started to follow me to my house, but I turned around and shook my head. I wasn't in the mood to talk to anyone right now.

He stopped and backed up a step. Disappointment was etched all over his face. "I'll call you later, then?"

"Okay."

Aly already went in, but I stopped right by the front door and watched Jake walk home by himself. His hands shoved into his pockets and his head downturned. I wanted to call him back. But I didn't. I didn't deserve to be happy right now.

By the time I got into the house and into my room, Aly had already washed her face and changed into her teal pajamas. Her bangs were a bit damp even though she had her hair held off her face with a headband. With a raised eyebrow, she sat there right in the center of the room on my squishy purple chair, waiting for me.

"Well?"

"Well . . . I'm feeling kind of hungry. Do you want some ramen?" I jabbed my thumb over my shoulder. "I could whip some up."

"Nice try. I already checked, and you're out of ramen. I did bring up a glass of water for you." She nodded toward the cup on my nightstand. "Figured you'd be thirsty after all the smooching and lying to yourself."

"Ouch. Were you thinking of that burn all night?"

A smile played at the corner of her lips. "I thought of it during the car ride."

With a reluctant laugh, I slid to the floor and stretched out on the carpet, arms and legs straight out like a starfish. "I'm exhausted."

"I don't blame you. Tonight was ... intense. But I'm still annoyed that you didn't tell me how you really felt about Jake." She paused. "I mean, we are best friends. And it's not like I didn't ask you a bunch of times."

My eyes focused on a dark paint smudge right by the ceiling fan. "I didn't tell you because I didn't *know* how I felt about him. At least not until recently. Like really recently." Finally, I lifted my head to look at her—giving her my best shot at puppy-dog eyes.

Shaking her head, Aly crossed her long legs beneath her. "You know, it's pretty obvious that Jake likes you. And if it wasn't before, it should be pretty clear to you after tonight. I seriously don't see what the problem is. You like him. I know you do. At least I hope you do after that show you guys pulled tonight."

My cheeks burst with heat. I climbed to my feet and folded my blanket just to have something to do with my hands, even though I hadn't folded my blanket in months. What was the point when it was just going to get messed up again in less than an hour? "Liking him isn't the problem. The problem is I don't know *how* to be in a relationship with Jake."

Aly's brows wrinkled. "Okay, I'm confused. Haven't you two already been in one for the past couple of weeks?"

With a sigh, I flopped back onto my bed with my hand slung over my eyes. "You know we just faked this whole dating thing to get our moms off of our backs. But underneath all of this, we're still the same people we've always been. He's Jake and I'm me. We've hated and annoyed each other practically our whole lives. In fact, we only did this because we wanted to get out of each other's lives. And now...what? We just forget about our whole plan just because of these last two weeks?"

"Yeah, your timing isn't the best. Look, there can be a million reasons for you guys not to date, but the bottom line is that you two like each other now. You. Like. Each. Other. That's all that really matters, so stop complaining." She flicked my forehead with two fingers, making me yelp. "Now, tomorrow you go straighten things out with Ben and *then* talk to Jake. Problem solved, and you can live happily ever after. Or at least until prom."

Rubbing my forehead with a wince, I groaned. She made everything sound so simple sometimes. "Since you seem to have all the answers, can you go talk to everyone for me? Especially Ben? Please?"

"Nope. Your relationships. You deal with them." Aly pulled open one of my facial masks and applied it to her face with a sigh, dismissing me and my problems. "That's what you get for being in love."

If that was true, it's starting to feel like more trouble than it's worth. But she was right. If I wanted to be with Jake—and deep down, I knew that I did—then I had to do whatever it took to fix this mess. To make a fresh start.

Tomorrow.

MIA

WITH MY PHONE IN ONE HAND to check the time, I jogged toward the old Milton Elementary schoolyard. The back of my flip-flops slapped against the pavement and the heels of my feet.

Jake was already sitting on the end of the slide at the playground. His feet kicked at the sand until billows of dust swirled around. I could already see his white sneakers turning gray and brown.

Something had to be wrong if he didn't care about his shoes getting dirty. He was the only person I knew who kept wet wipes in his car to clean his shoes.

Still, his face brightened as soon as he spotted me. He leaned forward, resting his chin on his clasped hands. That adorable half smile was already on his face. In return, I immediately got butterflies in my stomach. Especially the longer his gaze was on me, sweeping from the top of my head to the bottom of my feet and back again.

Even though there was a bit of a breeze, I could feel myself getting all warm and tingly.

It wasn't my fault, though. This was the first time we had seen each other since the festival. Okay, so that was only yesterday, but still, I couldn't stop the wave of nerves that washed over me.

Bracing one hand against the edge of the slide, I tried to play it cool. "So, you wanted to see me?"

His left brow rose. "You mean you didn't *want* to see me?"

"I don't know. Do you *want* me to *want* to see you?" I cringed inside. Gah, I was *not* used to flirting. Especially with Jake. Insulting him, yes. An occasional witty comeback to get the last word in, yes. But flirting? No way.

I felt like Jake could see right through my brain, scrambling to figure out a coy answer. And failing miserably.

He let out a short laugh as he reached out to touch my arm. "To be honest, I want a lot of things. But at the top of the list is that I always want to see you."

Oh, God. When did Jake get so darn swoony? It was like he was taking lessons from my favorite K-dramas.

My arm buckled a bit from his touch and slid off the slide. I was inches away from smacking the side of my face against the metal side before Jake jumped up and grabbed me.

"Are you okay?"

I waved my hand. "Yeah, just lost my balance. The sun was in my eyes. Made me dizzy or something."

He glanced up at the sky. The clouds were so thick that we could barely see where the sun was. Then he tugged on my hand until I came closer to his side. "Uh, sure, why don't we sit on the swings instead?"

Nodding, I followed him to the swing set on the other side of the playground. There were two little infant ones for the daycare and four regular ones.

Jake stopped right by the ones for the babies. He held out his other hand. "Do you need a boost? I don't want you to topple over again because I'm so handsome . . ."

I glared at him and knocked his hand away. "Ha ha. Did I ever tell you how funny you are?"

He blinked innocently at me. "Nope. Not in the fifteen years we've known each other."

"Good. I don't like to lie."

Snorting out loud, Jake waited until I sat on one of the normal swings before sitting on the one to my right. He sat the opposite way though so that we faced each other as we swung.

Our legs pumped back and forth as we got higher and higher, perfectly in sync. That's because we'd been on these swings a hundred times before. Racing to see who could get higher. I was lighter, but Jake's long legs gave him an advantage.

"About our breakup." My heart sank at the word, and I

stared down at the ground. "I know we were supposed to do it today, but—"

With wide yes, I glanced over at him. "But?"

He slowed down until his swing almost came to a complete stop. "I was hoping that you wanted to, maybe, forget about it? Just continue dating . . . for real?"

"Do . . . do you really want to give *us* a try? For real? Would we even work out?"

"Maybe not. The odds are definitely not in our favor. But . . ."

Hope crept up my stomach. "But?"

He looked down and let out a deep breath. "But what I learned these past few weeks is that I'd rather go through the craziness and arguing with you than a quiet boring life without you. It's not the same when you're not around. I'm not *me* when you're not around."

His words melted away any insecurity I felt. All of the reasons why we shouldn't be together disappeared just like that. They felt insignificant and small. I think I knew in my heart that everything he said was true. That I felt the exact same way. I just needed to hear him say the words.

"Gee, you're not so bad, either, Jake," he said in a high-pitched voice. "Don't have anything to say?"

With a laugh, my foot kicked out in his direction. "You already said everything that needs to be said."

The expression on his face turned a bit serious. "And what

about you? Have you said everything that needs to be said? Have you talked to Ben?"

I winced. "No, I tried, but I keep getting his voice mail. And *this* isn't exactly something I wanted to explain over text."

The metal rungs squeaked as he turned. "And what exactly did you want to explain to him?"

My toes dug into the sand until the tips of my flip-flops were buried. "You're really going to make me spell it out? The kiss. Us. About how we . . ."

"We . . . ?" He grinned. "I'm just messing with you."

I smacked my forehead with the palm of my hand. "I don't know what's wrong with me. Why the heck do I like you? You're still neurotic and crazy sometimes."

"That's true. And you're still messy most of the time. But you're still really pretty even when you're messy." A twinkle came into his eyes as he turned in the swing, twisting the rungs, to face me. The side of his face pressed against the metal. "And I like you anyway. So, are we starting over, then? Do we need to reintroduce ourselves?"

With a snort, I shook my head. "I don't think we need to start over quite that much. I mean, there's just too much that I know about you. The good, the bad, and the horrible."

"I bet there's one thing you don't know." Jake leaned forward. A smile played on the edges of his lips. "You don't know that I've been dying to kiss you again since the other night."

With a grin, I reached out and grabbed the metal chain on his swing to pull myself closer to him. To get easier access. "I did know that."

We both inched closer and closer to each other until the side of my thigh pressed against his. Each of us held on to the other swing's side to steady ourselves.

"You better make this better than our first kiss."

He slid his other hand around the nape of my neck. I could feel his warm breath on my cheek. Across my lips. "Yes, ma'am."

Both of us were smiling when our lips touched. His hands cradled my face and the nape of my neck. My fingertips pressed into his forearms and shoulders like I couldn't get close enough. Each of his kisses made me want more.

It was crazy how we had spent almost our whole lives resenting each other's company and now we were scrambling to get just a tiny bit closer.

But this time was different. There was a comfort in this kiss beneath the passion and heat. This time it was just for Jake and me. Because we liked each other and that was all that mattered.

After what felt like an eternity, when we finally broke apart, I was somehow off my swing and sitting on Jake's lap, arms wrapped around his shoulders and both legs straddling his lap. What the hell? Did I teleport over here or something?

His fingertips traced a line up and down my arm. "I think

we should go home before we get carried away. And I'm pretty sure this playground is far too innocent for that to happen."

"I don't know. This playground has seen its fair share of relationships." My fingers played with the dark locks curling around his ears. "You remember when I married Ian McCavery underneath that oak tree in first grade?"

He scowled. "No, where was I?"

"Actually, maybe you were sick with the flu that week. The one and only time I didn't get sick with you." I patted his shoulder with a smirk. "Don't worry, our marriage ended the next day when he wouldn't share his Pringles with me."

"Then he's an idiot." He paused. "Wait, what kind of Pringles were they?"

"Sour cream and onion."

"Oh, never mind, then. He made the right choice." Jake groaned when I smacked his shoulder this time, nearly dropping me as he squirmed on the swing. "Kidding! I'm kidding!"

"You better be." Unable to help myself, I kissed his cheeks, once on each side. "Let's go home."

OUR HANDS WERE SWINGING back and forth between us as we walked. It was quiet the whole walk home, but this time I didn't mind. It was a comfortable sort of silence. We communicated the whole time with tiny glances and finger strokes. His thumb caressed my knuckles to the inside of my wrist. I traced a heart shape into his palm and he squeezed my hand tightly in response.

It was pretty much as awesome as it sounds.

We were almost by our houses when I noticed the unfamiliar car in front of Jake's house. Mom and Mrs. Adler had dinner parties once in a while, but those were always at our house. Mrs. Adler rarely had people over at their house.

As we got closer and closer to the house, I noticed there were several people on the porch. Recognizing Mom's and Mrs. Adler's silhouettes in an instant, it took me a little while to figure out who the third person was. It must have hit Jake the exact same time it hit me because our arms immediately stopped swinging and all Jake could do was stare. We both did.

He was a little bigger than I remembered. Especially around the shoulders. He used to be lean and tall like Jake, but it looked like he must have been hitting the gym or something on the cruise ship. The curly dark hair and the easy smile were still the same. Although it wavered a bit when he turned to us.

It was Finn.

JAKE

I COULD FEEL MIA'S hand squeeze mine tighter, but I couldn't look at her. I just kept staring like an idiot as Finn came down the steps and closer to us. He stopped when he was a few feet away.

"Hi, Jake. Hey, Mia." He shoved his hands in his pockets. "It's been a while."

I froze at the sight of him. A thousand things raced through my head, but all I could do was stand there and blink at him. "What are you—How—" I could barely get any words out.

He looked over his shoulder nervously. "I just got in an hour ago. Mom told me that you were out with Mia—"

My jaw tightened at the casual way he said "Mom." "No, I meant why are you *here*?"

"Oh, I came home to visit. Didn't Mia tell you?"

Uh, wait, what? I turned to stare at her, and she shook her

head frantically. "I don't know what he's talking about. I swear, I didn't know that he was coming at all."

Finn took a couple of steps toward us, slowly like we were a pair of baby deer. "I emailed you about it yesterday. You didn't get it?"

I expected her to deny it again, but instead, her eyes just widened. "I didn't check my email yet. A lot has been going on since . . . yesterday."

I dropped her hand like it was a bomb. My chest churned uncomfortably as I turned to face her. "Wait, email? What— are you guys friends or something? Have you been in contact this whole time? And you didn't tell me?"

"No, it's only been a few emails the last two weeks. I swear, I—" She reached out to touch my arm, but I jerked away. Her hand grasped the air between us for another second or two before it fell to her side. "Jake, I'm sorry. I just wanted to help."

"Did I ever ask you for help?" My voice shook a bit as I raked my hands through my hair, trying to figure out what the hell was going on. And I couldn't stop staring at Mia for an explanation. "How did you even get each other's emails?"

With a quick glance in Mia's direction, Finn raised a hand. "It was—"

"It was me," she admitted in a small voice. Her head dropped even lower. "I saw his emails on your laptop and copied down his email address."

"But I was the one who continued it. I kept pestering her

to tell me how you and Mom were doing," Finn explained. "How your lives have been."

My jaw was rigid and tight as I looked back and forth at the two of them. I almost wished that Mia had lied and said it was Finn who emailed her first. Then I wouldn't have felt so betrayed by her. I would have less of a reason to be pissed at her. I could have tried to let it go. I could have . . .

"You knew how I felt about Finn," I said in a low voice. "You knew what it was like when he left. You. Knew."

Finally, she looked up at me. Her eyes were shining with unshed tears. "I know, and I'm sorry. I just thought it was the right thing to do. I thought that if Finn knew how you were doing, that he would come back. And then you two could make up and—"

"Stop. Just stop." Every word she said just made me shake with frustration. In fact, just looking at them standing there together like a team made my jaw clench together until my teeth started to ache. Finally, I couldn't take it anymore and had to turn away. "I don't want to hear anything from either of you anymore."

I tried to storm into the house, but Mom and Mrs. Le blocked my way. "Come on, Jake, just give him a chance."

"Give him a chance?" I laughed in disbelief and shook my head. They must be crazy. "Seriously? Did it ever occur to anyone that there was a *reason* I never emailed Finn back? Because I didn't want to give any of *this* a chance. In fact, this is the last thing I want. Hell, I went through this whole fake dating thing just so I wouldn't have to see his stupid face anymore."

Mom looked both sad and confused. "What are you—"

"Jake." Mia froze on the steps behind me and shook her head. "Don't do this."

"What? You mean tell the truth? Why not? We're all here. Might as well tell everyone. It's the right thing to do." I repeated her earlier words. Her face dropped, and I felt an ounce of satisfaction in my gut. "So guess what, Mom and Mrs. Le? This whole dating thing was just one huge lie that Mia and I thought up. We figured that if we pretended to date and then had a huge breakup, you two would finally get off our backs about being together. Because just telling you that we didn't want to be together for years wasn't a big enough hint to you."

Mom opened her mouth to say something, but I held up a hand to stop her. "And you know what the crazy thing is? Mia did it so she could date other guys, and I only went along with the crazy idea because I didn't want to go on the stupid cruise this summer. Because I didn't want to see him." My finger jabbed in Finn's direction. "Ironic, isn't it? So now that you know, it's all over. We're done pretending."

I looked from one shocked face to the next, and my satisfaction just grew. At least until I looked at Mia. She stared straight at me with a disappointed look as she hugged her arms to her chest. My mind immediately flashed back to just ten minutes ago when we were happy and kissing. When everything felt like it was perfect.

It felt like ages had passed since then.

Still, I shook my head and turned away from her, from everyone, to open the door. I paused for a moment without turning around. "So maybe you guys will finally believe me this time when I say that I don't want to 'give this a chance.' That I don't want to be part of this family. And I want you all to leave. Me. Alone."

I went up to my room and flopped down onto the bed without turning on the lights. Just laid there in the dark quiet room as I stared at the shadows on the ceiling. My head hurt like it was being crushed.

The front door opened and closed. A couple of minutes later, I heard them come up the stairs. There was low whispering outside my door for a few minutes, but the footsteps finally moved away from my room. First Mom's door creaked open and then Finn's down the hall. Until finally it was quiet. And I was alone. Just like I wanted to be.

It didn't make me any happier, though.

MIA

IT'D BEEN THREE DAYS, and I still hadn't had a chance to talk to Jake. I woke up early to catch him before school. Practically staked out in front of his locker in between classes. Even kept the shades of my window open so I could spot him. Nothing.

Gosh, if he was this good at avoiding me before, then our moms would have given up on us ages ago.

I didn't want to be one of those girls who drowned their sorrows in ice cream after they're dumped, but there was a reason that everyone did it in the movies and on TV. It was just comforting to eat something cool and sweet. Even if my heart wasn't happy, at least my stomach would be.

So I compromised and settled in bed with some mango sorbet from the Asian market. With a couple of green tea mochi tossed in. At least then I could half pretend I was being healthy.

Twisting the gold ring around my finger, I was halfway done with my second box of mochi and kind of feeling sluggish from all the sugar when Mom called me from downstairs. "Mia, someone's at the door for you!"

It was probably Aly. She told me she was going to come by to drag me out of the house before I got arrested for stalking. Although technically, was it even stalking when I was home? I was merely people watching. Watching a certain person.

I took my ice cream with me as I came downstairs. It wasn't until I opened the door that I realized it wasn't Aly outside. There was a male back on our front porch. With broad shoulders and dressed in jeans and a knitted polo. He turned around . . .

It was Ben.

Panicking, I slammed the door in his face. Then immediately smacked the top of my head with both hands for being such a wimp. It was stupid, but it was a reflex. Like ducking when someone threw a ball at you. If the ball was a handsome senior you sort of cheated on.

Just a few weeks ago, I would have killed to have some alone time with Ben. Like, would have fought in the Hunger Games kind of killed. But now Ben was pretty much the *last* person I wanted to see.

Finally letting out a deep breath, I put the box of mochis on the end table, redid my ponytail so it wasn't a lopsided mess anymore, and straightened my gray Flintstones T-shirt before opening the door again. "Hi, Ben. Sorry about . . . before. You caught me by surprise."

"It's okay." He shoved his hands in his pockets. His lips were set in a thin line. "Could I talk to you for a minute?"

"Uh, sure." I stepped out onto the porch but leaned against the closed front door with my hands clasped in front of me.

"So, Mia—"

"I'm so sorry, Ben, about the other night." I wrung my hands together until they started to hurt a bit. "I don't know what happened, but I swear that I didn't *mean* for any of it to happen. I would never have invited you if I did. What kind of monster do you think I am?"

"I don't—"

"Of course you don't think that. You're such a good guy. And perfect. Have I ever told you how perfect you are? Like perfect with a capital *P.* Handsome. Smart. Sexy as hell. Like seriously, daaamn." I stretched out the last word into a couple of syllables to really drive the point home. "Any girl would be thrilled to be with you. Any girl who isn't stupid like me. Apparently. Because I am that stupid."

Ben held up a hand to shut me up. "As much as I love hearing how awesome I am, I think it's my turn now. I just want to say one thing, and then I'm going to go."

Now I felt even more ashamed than before. Here I was rambling on and on to make myself feel better when I didn't have the decency to go to Ben first. I mean, I tried to the first day, but after Finn showed up . . . I was so occupied with Jake that I completely forgot about Ben.

I let out a deep breath. "You're right. Let me have it."

He shoved his hand into his hair and looked down at our feet. "I'm not going to lie, when I saw you and Jake together, I was pissed. Really pissed."

"I know and I'm sorry—"

"Just let me finish, okay? I need to get this out." Ben shook his head like he was still confused. "I know we were just getting to know each other, but I *really* liked you. And I thought you felt the same way. I even talked to the director about staying in town after graduation so I would be around. And then . . . to see you kissing Jake. After I asked you a bunch of times if there was anything going on. I just felt so . . . so . . ."

I winced and prepared myself.

He stopped and took a couple of deep breaths. "But I thought about it the past couple of days and . . . it's okay."

"It's—wait, what?" I stood there and blinked at him like an idiot. "How could it be okay? I was kissing another guy. You should be yelling at me."

He let out a soft laugh. "I've never been good at yelling at girls, so I think I'll pass. Like I said, we weren't official or anything. And deep down, I should have known there was something going on between you two. You were in your own special little bubble that no one could join. I just didn't want to admit it because I liked you so much."

My heart wrenched at his words. But I didn't know how to respond. "Sorry" didn't seem like enough and besides, anything I said now wouldn't make anything better. All I could do was hang my head in shame.

"So anyway, that's all I wanted to say." Ben took a step toward me before stopping himself and backing up. "I'll see you at rehearsal."

"Okay." He was halfway down the steps when I called him again. "Ben? I just wanted to say that I really am sorry, though. Truly, truly sorry."

His face was still sad, but he managed a tiny smile. "I know."

And then, just like that, he was gone.

I always knew that Ben was great, but I never realized until now that he was such an amazing guy. Even though I put him through all of that, he still came to sort of give me his blessing and—Oh my God, he was the Second Lead Syndrome. My life had suddenly officially turned into a K-drama.

Not to mention, I ruined my relationship with Jake and now I was all alone.

With a loud groan, I sank down on the top step and rubbed at my temples with both hands.

A couple of minutes went by until the front door creaked open. Mom came out onto the porch and handed me my box. "I figured you'd want this back."

"Thanks." The mochi was all melted by now, and I poked my finger at the gooey green mixture.

She hesitated for a few minutes before sitting down beside me. "Who was that boy?"

"It's . . . a really long story."

"Does he have anything to do with why you and Jake pretended to date in the first place?"

"Sort of. We were kind of seeing each other, but Jake and I—" To my surprise, tears sprang to my eyes, and I blinked rapidly to make them go away. Wailing about it wasn't going to make things better. All it would do is make my eyes swollen. Although puffy eyes were the least of my problems right now. "It doesn't even matter now because there isn't a Jake and I. Not anymore. And it's all because of me. If I hadn't been nosy and butted in when I shouldn't have. I ruined everything."

"Oh, honey." Mom wrapped an arm around my shoulders and hugged me. "You didn't. You did what you thought was right. Hell, I think what you did was amazing. You brought Finn home."

"But I still shouldn't have gone behind Jake's back."

"That's true, but you did it for him. I'm sure he will understand with time."

I glanced up at her. "But if he doesn't, then that means all of our family stuff . . . the Adlers won't be in our lives anymore. At least not like they were. Are you okay with that?"

She looked wistful. "It's fine. You're more important to me."

"Aren't you mad that we lied to you about dating, though?"

Mom's body grew rigid and she glanced down at me with a guilty look on her face. "Honestly, Mrs. Adler and I knew that you two were lying about dating ages ago."

I pulled out of her embrace, momentarily forgetting about Jake. "Uh, what?"

"Well, we did believe you at first. But once we started talking about it, we realized it was too convenient. Too easy. Plus, you two aren't as great at lying as you think you are."

"But . . ." I shook my head as I tried to figure things out. "But if you knew, why did you two go along with it?"

She swept her dark hair over her shoulder. "Well, we were going to call you out on it, but I realized that this way you two would actually willingly spend time together. And be a couple. Which was a step closer than anything we've ever thought of to get you two together, so we decided to just play along. And if you two decided to break up afterward, then at least we gave it our best shot."

I stared at her for another few seconds before laughing. An uncontrollable laugh that just burst out and I couldn't do anything to stop it. Mom just sat there and watched me with a confused look on her face, which only made me laugh even harder. Tears came to my eyes, and I wiped at them over and over again until the only thing left was my tears.

I just couldn't believe that we got played by our moms.

We thought we were being so clever. All the things we did, the PDAs, the pet names, everything was all for nothing. Because they were laughing at us the entire time.

Damn.

And now here we were, finally getting what we had been longing for years for, and now everyone was miserable. Especially us.

"Sounds like you're having a blast. Can I join you?" Aly asked, walking toward us with a large tote bag over her shoulder.

"Did you come to yell at me?"

She shook her head. "Nope. I've decided that if you're determined to mope, then I'll sit here and mope with you. I already ordered the pizza and picked up some caramel popcorn and nut mix. Plus, I wrote out a list of the top-five most tragic K-drama romances. After a couple of hours of watching cancer scares, overbearing mother-in-laws, birth secrets, and angsty fights in the rain, everything will seem much better."

I couldn't help laughing as I wiped at the tears on my face. "You promise?"

"Of course. Everything will work out eventually." Aly hugged me before lifting her head to grin at me. "I swear on my Netflix account that everything will be back to normal in a month."

A reluctant smile tugged at my lips. "Are you sure you want to do that? Holidays are coming up."

"That just shows you how certain I am that everything will be okay."

I wished I could be as certain about everything as Aly was. But at least I knew that no matter what, I'd still have Mom and Aly on my side. And that wasn't too bad at all.

JAKE

I SCOWLED WHEN I walked into the kitchen and found Finn sitting by the counter with a big dopey smile on his face. Ever since he came home, he had been everywhere. In the bathroom when I woke up. Hanging out in the hall right before I went to sleep. Cleaning out the garage when I came home from school. I was basically tripping over him every freaking step I took. It was like the dude had nothing better to do with his time except annoy me.

"Morning!" he called out, waving a spoon at me before scooping up more cereal into his mouth. "Do you want some Froot Loops or Frosted Flakes?"

I grabbed some orange juice from the fridge. "Neither. I don't eat breakfast in the morning."

"Since when?"

"Since three days ago."

Finn snorted. "You got sarcastic these past two years. I like it."

"Like I give a shit about what you like." I downed the glass of OJ in one gulp and put the glass into the sink. "Why don't you just leave us alone and go back to your dumb little cruise ship? That's what you're good at. Leaving. It's not like Mom and I matter to you anyway."

"That's not true."

"Yeah, right."

He laced both hands together behind his neck and leaned back in his chair. "It isn't, but I know you won't believe anything I say anyway so what's the point?"

"Exactly, so you should just leave."

"No, I'm not going anywhere. Not until you've said everything you need to say. Even if you won't listen to me, I'm going to listen to you."

God, why was he so freaking stubborn? I crossed my arms and stared at the ceiling in frustration. "There isn't anything left to say."

Finn rolled his eyes. "Come on. You're not this much of an ass because you don't have anything to say. I disappeared on you and Mom for two years. Without even saying goodbye. Just texted Mom when I was already past the Texas state line. You're pissed at me. Just admit it. Unless you're too much of a chicken to actually say it out loud."

My jaw tightened, and I had to grip the edge of the counter

behind me so I wouldn't go over there and deck him. "I'm not a chicken. I just don't see the point in talking to you. I haven't for two years. Why start now?"

Finn got up and moved toward the doorway so I wouldn't leave. His hand still held on to the spoon in one hand like it was a weapon. "You were really chatty a few days ago on the front porch in front of everyone. Now that it's just you and me, you don't have anything left to say? Fine, then I'll start talking first." He let out a deep breath before dropping the hand with the spoon. "I'm sorry for leaving the way that I did. I was a coward and a jerk for ditching you."

I rolled my eyes. "Whatever. I don't care what you say."

"Come on, Jake. I'm begging you to just talk to me. Do it for Mom's sake."

I don't know if it was because he mentioned Mom, but the anger pushed up from my gut and made everything in front of me get blurry. This was enough. "Fine, you want me to talk? I'll talk." Pushing away from the sink, I jerked my arm back and punched him straight in his jaw.

He stumbled back and dropped the spoon onto the floor. His right hand rubbed his jaw, and he just stared at me with a confused expression.

For some reason, this only made me angrier, and I shoved his shoulders. Twice. "Don't you dare talk about Mom like you care about her. If you did, then you wouldn't have ever left her, you jackass. She gave up her whole life to raise us, and you just abandoned her. Abandoned both of us. Did you even care that she cried herself to sleep at night for weeks after you left? I still remember hearing her through the walls even though she didn't do it until she thought I was asleep. Like I could actually sleep after you left. Like I—"

My arm moved back to punch Finn again, but he didn't move. He just stood there and watched my fist move toward his face. His eyes even squeezed together as he waited for the punch, but he didn't flinch.

At the very last second, I froze and let my hand drop to my side. The anger zapped out of me, and the only thing left was exhaustion. "I don't even remember our real parents. They died so long ago. All I've known my whole life is you and Mom. And Mom is great, I love her, but it was just you and me. You were the only one I had growing up. You looked out for me. We understood each other. We were there for each other. And then you just left without saying anything. Do you know how much that hurt?"

I took a couple of steps back away from him and leaned against the wall. "I mean, our parents left us, but it wasn't their choice. But you . . . you chose to not be a part of my life anymore. You chose to not be there for me anymore."

With a guilty look on his face, Finn let out a deep sigh and shook his head. "I know, and I'm sorry. I was just—no, I'm not going to make excuses for what I did. It was wrong and stupid, and I'm really, really sorry."

I swallowed at the lump in my throat and turned away. "Like I said, it doesn't matter now. Mom and I have been getting along fine without you. So it would have been better if you just stayed away forever. Why did you have to come back and drag Mia down to your level?"

"I dragged Mia down? Do you even—" To my disbelief, he stood there and *laughed* at me. "I know that I've been stupid, but right now, you're being almost as stupid as I was."

"What?"

"You broke her heart, dude. You made her fall in love with you, and then you broke it."

"Nothing's going on between us," I said firmly. "We were just pretending to date so Mom and Mrs. Le would stop hounding us. It wasn't real. And now it's over."

"Mia didn't go behind your back with the intention of betraying you. She did all of this to help you. To make you happy. Just think of it this way, if she didn't care about you, then she wouldn't have even bothered."

When I didn't respond, Finn rolled his eyes and pushed past me toward the kitchen table to grab his laptop. "Damn it, I can even prove it. In every single email, all she talks about is you and how great you are. And how she just wishes you could be happy. Look, I don't know anything about your relationship or fake relationship or whatever the heck you two had going on, but it doesn't take a rocket scientist to figure out that she is head over heels in love with you for real."

I knew he was just baiting me, but I couldn't help asking. "Really?" But before he could answer, I shook my head. "It doesn't matter now. She shouldn't have emailed you in the first place. Should have just kept her nose out of it. Not like I believe anything you say anyway."

"You don't need to believe me. You can see for yourself." He shoved the open laptop into my chest. "Just read Mia's emails, and then we'll talk some more, you big baby. Once you know the whole story. And if you still want to yell at me, then that's fine, but only *after* you read her emails."

EMAILS

Hi, Finn!

The cruise ship sounds like a magical place. Maybe someday Mom and I will be able to go. It'll be especially great if we could also get a discount. I don't know if you'll be able to pull any strings, but if you could, then definitely count us in! I mean, yeah, I got sick a few times when Mom's ex would take Jake and me fishing, but I'm sure I'll be fine on the cruise ship.

    I didn't know that you kept in touch with Mrs. Adler. Jake never mentioned it to me, but maybe he doesn't know, either. Actually, I'm pretty sure that he doesn't. I know that Jake and your mom don't talk about you very much. He doesn't *really talk about you to any of us, but I could tell that he thinks about you. Sometimes he would drum his fingers on the dinner table like you used to do back then. I don't think he realizes that he does, but I noticed that he started doing it after you left. It was really annoying at first, but after a while, you get used to it.*

To be honest, it was pretty rough around here after you left. Mom took Mrs. Adler out every day to keep her busy, but Jake ... well, he just stayed inside and watched TV all day long. It didn't matter what was on. Game shows. News. Cartoons. He would just stare blankly at the screen for hours. Didn't even clean up the chip crumbs off of the couch. I swear, he didn't even change for a couple of days. I'd never seen him like that before.

After a few days, I had to pretend that Mom sent me to your house every day just to keep an eye on him. Plus ... I didn't want him to be alone.

Look, I don't know what your reason for leaving is, and I'm not going to ask. All I want to know is if you'll ever be coming back. Because you're missing out on being in Jake's life. And I would kill you if you ever told anyone this, but he's a pretty awesome person to get to know.

Plus, we just got this new bubble tea place that opened up right next to Royal House. Jake and I just went there after dim sum, and it's really delicious. You should really come try it out. My treat.

—Mia

Hey, Mr. Superstar,

The YouTube videos of your performance last month were great! Somehow you look different, but still exactly the same. Guess two years away from home can do that to you. I, however, look completely different now even though I haven't left Texas and am way prettier than before. Seriously. If you want to see for yourself, then just hop home to check!

Jake has been basically the same. Home. School. Work. So the usual. We went to eat dinner and watched a movie earlier today with a couple of friends. I know, how exciting, right?

Although there's this music festival thing next week that Rose has been trying to get Jake to perform at, but he still won't go. He claims that he's not interested in music anymore, but I could tell that's a bunch of crap. How can someone with so much talent like him just not care? Don't tell him this, but I still watch your old videos singing together online sometimes. His voice soothes me.

I think he's honestly just scared of trying. It doesn't matter if I know he'll be awesome. I hope you don't mind, but I sent him the videos of you singing on the cruise ship. Just to see if it would spark something in him. He didn't say anything to me about it, but he also didn't yell at me, either, so I'd consider that a huge success! I'll try to talk to him a bit more about performing.

—Mia

_____

Hey,

I just wanted to write you a quick email and let you know that Jake decided to perform at the festival after all! Isn't that awesome?

I'm actually getting ready now so he can come pick me up so we can head out. I'm not sure exactly what changed his mind. Could be your videos or could be my pushing, but who knows?

(Although I'm pretty sure it's all me.) I'm just glad that he's actually giving it a shot. He deserves to be happy. Plus, he's super talented, so there's no reason that he should hide it from the world. Everyone will love him.

Anyway, I'll try to record the performance and send it to you later tonight!

—Mia

I READ THROUGH ALL the emails over and over for the next hour. Lingered over every word. Every paragraph.

I could almost imagine Mia sitting on her bed as she wrote each email. Her legs crossed as her face scrunched up in concentration. Probably had a bag of chips on the nightstand next to her to munch on.

Finn was still sitting in the kitchen when I came back down, this time sipping a can of soy milk Mom got from the Asian market with Mrs. Le last week. There was a smug smile on his face as he watched me. "So?"

His smile was annoying, but I couldn't help ducking my head a bit when I slid the laptop back to him. "Maybe you're right. It's not entirely her fault."

"Nope. So, what are you going to do about it?"

That was a hard question. I wasn't sure what I wanted to do. On one hand, I was still mad at her for going behind my back. On the other hand, after reading those emails, I couldn't blame her for what she did. Especially when I still missed her like crazy. It'd only been a few days, but I already missed her chattering and laughter. Her stealing my food and fiddling with my radio. Once, I started to say something to her in the car before realizing that she wasn't there. I don't know how I ever imagined life without her.

"I don't know yet," I finally said.

Finn looked sympathetic as he pushed the laptop to the side. "Well, an apology would probably be a good start. And don't wait too long, or it won't work anymore."

"Like you waited two years to give your apology?"

"Yeah, about that." He glanced down at his hands. "I'm still not making any excuses, but I just want you to know that I didn't leave because I didn't care about you. I left because—because . . ."

"Because?" Mom suddenly appeared out of nowhere and leaned against the kitchen doorframe. She was still in her pajamas and bedroom slippers. The ones that I bought for her for Mother's Day last year. "As glad as I am to have you back, I've been waiting for this answer for years, but I was always too afraid to ask."

Finn shifted back and forth in his seat like he was cornered, and I couldn't help smiling in satisfaction. Crossing my arms, I tilted my chair back to lean on two legs and watched him squirm.

"I don't know. I guess the easiest way to explain it is . . . honestly, I was feeling trapped at home. I had been for a while actually. I was tired of being the kid who survived the car accident. The one that had to live up to our dead parents' expectations." Sighing, he ran both of his hands through his hair, tugging it a bit in frustration. "I know it sounds stupid. Even I didn't understand what I was feeling. I just felt *suffocated* and knew I had to leave. Get away. Once I did, I knew it was a horrible mistake. But I was too ashamed to come back."

I didn't think anything Finn said would have made me forgive him, and I still didn't. But I did start to feel bad for him. I never knew he felt that way. I always thought everything was perfectly fine. Then again, I didn't remember Mom and Dad at all, so it never bothered me whenever people brought them up. I was barely two when they passed, but Finn was already five. Old enough to know what was going on. Old enough to miss them. And I guess it affected him more than I thought. More than any of us knew.

"Oh, honey." Mom patted his shoulder. "You should have told me you felt that way. All this time, I thought it was something that I did. That I was . . . lacking as a mom. That I disappointed you both."

We both stared at her in horror. "How could you think—"

"Why would you—" Finn hugged Mom. "You and Jake are the reasons I wanted to come back. But I didn't know how you would react. If you would forgive me. It took a while, but Mia told me that if I didn't come back now, then I would be losing my family forever. And I was a fucking idiot if I let that happen. Sorry, Mom."

I stared at Finn. "She did? I didn't see that email."

"Yeah, it was the second or third email. I..." He cleared his throat. "Accidentally deleted it." He shook his head and laughed. "I don't know how she managed to pull off nagging in an email, but she did. And she knows quite a few curse words."

Mom gasped, but I just laughed, already imagining how that particular email would have sounded.

"Well, whatever she said, I'm glad that she did." She rubbed her forehead against the top of Finn's head like she did when we were kids. "I've missed having both of you in the house."

"Me too, Mom."

They stayed like that for a few minutes, and I couldn't help feeling a tad bit happy. As mad as I was, Mom was right. It felt good to have Finn and Mom together again.

With their heads still pressed together, they both turned to me with expectant smiles. "What?"

"Now it's your turn to confess something," Finn said, as if it was my turn to wash the dishes or something.

"I don't have anything to confess."

Mom rolled her eyes. "You're a teenage boy. You pretended to date someone only to fall in love with her. Don't deny it. I know you did. And then you broke up with her. And now your estranged brother of two years just came back into your life. Are you sure you don't have anything else to get off your chest?"

God, when she put it like that . . .

"I already said everything I needed to say to Finn."

He shook his head. "No, you didn't. There's more. I could feel it."

Jeez. Finn comes home for a few days, and suddenly he's all intuitive and insightful. And the worst part was that Mom was buying into this whole thing.

I shrugged and kept my mouth shut. Mom and Finn gave each other knowing looks and leaned back in their chairs before crossing their arms. Minutes passed, but no one said anything and all you heard was the *tick tock* of the clock on the wall.

Surrendering, I let out a deep sigh. "Fine. I already said that I'm pissed at you for leaving and ditching Mom and me."

"And?"

"And, I guess, I ended up having to pick up the slack. I had to be the man of the house and do *whatever* I could to make her happy." My voice got louder and louder, and I was just getting started. Taking in a deep breath, I let out all the anger that was bubbling to the surface. "You're off doing whatever you want to, but I'm stuck here."

Even I was surprised with everything I was saying, but it was as if once I started, I couldn't stop. I would have continued,

281

but Mom wrapped me in a tight hug. Crap, was she crying? My shoulder and sleeve were rapidly getting soaked. I didn't mean to make her cry. I knew it. I shouldn't have said anything. "No, Mom, I didn't mean that. I just—"

"No, you listen to me, Jake Nathaniel Adler. It is *not* your job to keep me happy. It's *my* job to make sure that you're happy. And healthy. And to live your life however you want to." Her fist pounded on my back with every sentence she said. And it hurt. "That's the only way I'll really be happy. That's what I signed on for when I brought you two home, and I've never regretted it for a minute."

"But . . . I don't even know what I want anymore."

"Then you just have to figure it out together." She finally pulled away from me and smiled at Finn. "All three of us will figure out what we want from now on. Like a family. Okay?"

Finn glanced over at me, waiting for my answer. To be honest, I was still worried that he would disappear on us again, but for Mom's sake, I caved. "Okay."

With a sparkling smile, she ruffled the top of our heads affectionately. "How about we celebrate being together? Go out for lunch." She backed up toward the hall. "I have to make a few calls, but I'll get ready in an hour. Okay?"

"Sure."

Nodding in agreement, I grabbed the cereal box from him and poured myself a huge bowl, suddenly starving.

Finn washed the few dishes in the sink before turning

around to face me. He wiped his hands on a white towel. "I saw your performance at the festival last weekend."

I paused midpour. "Oh, yeah?"

"Yeah, you were good. Really good." He laughed. "I almost didn't recognize you at first. I know you said that you didn't know what you wanted to do, but I really think you should continue with the music thing."

Avoiding his eyes, I concentrated on pouring the rest of my cereal. I wanted to not care, but his opinion still mattered to me no matter what. "I don't know . . ."

"You don't have to do it my way. Stay here. Take some music classes; just don't give it up."

Not knowing how to respond, I nodded again and took a big bite of the cereal.

He sat down hard on the stool across the island from me. His fingers tapped on the countertop. "I still need to get back to the cruise ship for the rest of the year, but I'm thinking of maybe trying the college route. Mom said you were thinking of going to University of Houston? I've already contacted the dean of admission about my application for next year."

I choked on the Frosted Flakes, and Finn had to smack my back several times to clear my throat. Between his and Mom's hits today, I wouldn't be surprised if my back was black and blue by now.

"You can't—you can't actually be planning on going to college with me, right?"

"Might as well since we'll be roomies again." He reached over and pulled me into a headlock like he used to when we were kids. "We could even carpool to classes together. Think of how much fun it'll be!"

I pinched his underarm until he let go. "God, in that case, I think I might go to community college instead."

"Point taken. Figured you'd want to be carpooling with Mia anyway. I don't want to be the third wheel."

"Right. About that . . ."

Finn leaned forward and lightly punched my shoulder with a crooked smile. "Let me give you a bit of advice, Little Bro. Don't let your pride get in the way before you lose her for good."

I eyed him. "Are you speaking from experience? Did you meet someone on the cruise ship?"

"And now the personal sharing time is over," he said without answering my questions. Finn got up and headed toward the doorway. "Don't say I didn't warn you, though. Girls like Mia don't stay available for long."

Damn it, what he said was starting to make sense. And it was really starting to annoy me. Especially since I was still really mad at both Mia and Finn. But I could already feel my anger with Finn starting to fade. Just a tiny bit. And the whole reason I was mad at Mia was because of him.

Then again, Mia wouldn't have been Mia if she didn't butt in and try to help. She instinctively knew what I needed before

I even did. Just like two years ago when she knew the last thing I wanted after Finn left was to talk. And now, she knew that I would finally be ready to listen to him.

But what if she was wrong? What if I wasn't actually ready?

With a sigh, I stirred the soggy cereal left in my bowl but didn't feel like taking another bite. Instead I dumped the rest of the cereal in the trash and washed the bowl before putting it away. I glanced over at the Les' house, and I could still see Mia's car parked in the driveway.

I understood exactly why she did it, but that didn't change the fact that she shouldn't have gone behind my back. I think that's what hurt the most. But the truth was, I missed her. A lot. And even though I was still mad, I wanted to see her again. Talk to her again.

Now the only problem was, how would I apologize without actually apologizing and looking like a total jerk?

MIA

I ALMOST TRIPPED on a pot of orchids as Mom pushed me out of the house. She was in such a hurry that she almost walked out of the house in her bedroom slippers. "Why do you have to drive me to school again? I thought your car was fixed."

Mom linked arms with me. "The craziest thing happened yesterday. I went into the garage to get my purse from my car, and the tire was completely flat! Like a pancake. Anyway, Finn said he'll come over to check it out later, but I need to run some errands first with Mrs. Adler. So I won't be driving you to school after all."

"But—"

"Don't worry, I already got you a ride."

Right on cue, Jake pulled up our driveway. The sunlight glinted off of his windshield as he and his mom climbed out of the car together. Shoving both hands in his pockets, he gave me a hesitant shrug. "I heard you needed a ride?"

Trying to hold in the smile that leaped to my lips at the sight of Jake, I glanced over at the guilty expression on Mom's face. "I thought you said you were done with all of this matchmaking."

With wide eyes, she held up both hands in surrender before dusting them off. "Oh, I am. This is the last thing we're going to do for you two. Get together. Don't get together. To be honest, we don't really care anymore. We're officially abandoning this Jakia ship once and for all."

Mrs. Adler came over to Mom and wrapped her arm around her waist. "That's right. We have better things to do with our lives instead of worrying about you two all the time. Not only are we best friends, but now we decided we want to be even more. We've decided we're going to be business partners."

Forgetting about Jake for a moment, I turned to look at Mom. Her face was bright with excitement. "Really?"

"Yep, Mrs. Adler is going to quit her job at the office and help me expand the wedding-planning business into a catering business, too."

"I always hated that place anyway. It's too cold and smells like old moldy papers." Mrs. Adler laughed with joy as she clapped her hands together in excitement. "Your mom and I are going to be very busy. Too busy to meddle in your lives. From now on, you're both on your own."

"Speaking of being busy," Mom said as she glanced down

at her watch and grabbed Mrs. Adler's wrist. "We have to leave now if we're going to make our meeting with the Whitmores."

"Right! Well, you kids have fun. We'll see you at dinner tonight."

Our moms zoomed out of there quicker than me during biology dissection day. Now that we were alone, Jake and I just stood there, awkwardly looking at each other out of the corners of our eyes.

Coughing in my fist, I kicked at a rock on the sidewalk between us. "I guess this means that you and Finn are okay now?"

He shielded his eyes from the sun and shrugged. "Not okay. But . . . we're getting there. I think."

I let out a sigh of relief. "I'm so glad. And I know that I already said it, but I'm so sorry I emailed Finn behind your back. I just thought that was what you needed. Which was stupid of me. How do I know what you need? I just know what I need, and I need to tell you how sorry—"

With a soft chuckle, Jake waved his hand in front of my face to make me stop. "You know what? I don't know about you, but I'm getting so annoyed with the word sorry. Aren't you?"

"To be honest, yeah. I've been saying that word a lot lately." I chewed on my lower lip and searched his face. "You're not mad at me anymore?"

"No, I still am. I mean, you were right. I did need to see Finn. To clear the air between us. But you still shouldn't have gone behind my back like that. You won't always be right." He let out a short laugh. "Plus, you're lucky that I like you too much to hold a grudge."

With a sigh of relief, I smiled. "But at least I'm right this time. And what about us? Are we . . . good?"

At first, he just stood there, staring at the ground, and I started to get nervous. Finally, he took three huge steps and wrapped his arms around my waist in response. "We're perfect. Jeez, I've missed you. Even when I was super annoyed with you, I missed you so much."

God, this felt so good. I leaned into his shoulder. My fingers played with the collar of his shirt. "I missed you, too. So, what now?"

He laced his fingers through mine and pulled me toward the street. "How about we take a walk?"

Huh? That was basically the last thing I expected him to say. "Now?"

"Yeah, I promise it'll be a short one."

". . . okay."

Jake wasn't lying about it being a short walk because we barely crossed the street before he stopped right in front of his house. Without letting go of me, he laid down in the middle of his lawn. He tried to tug me down with him, but I stayed upright. "What are you doing? We're going to be late for school."

He gave me a lazy grin that pulled at my heart. "Now look

who's being a Goody Two-Shoes. Come on, I just wanted to hang out for a bit. I think after everything we've been through these last few weeks, we deserve some time to ourselves."

Still confused, I sat down beside him. "What should we do now? Just sit here?"

"Now we can do whatever the hell we want for once. Maybe we should start with going on a real first date? With no nosy moms this time. Just you and me."

"You and me. That does sound nice. . . ." I slowly licked my lower lip and instantly his eyes slid downward. With a small grin, I slung both arms around his neck and pulled him closer. "Hmm, doing whatever the hell we want *does* sound nice. Where do you want to go?"

My lips almost reached his when he pulled back to grin at me. Lacing his hand through mine, he held up our entwined hands and kissed my fingers. Slowly. One by one. My stomach fluttered more and more with each kiss.

Finally, he kissed the little gold heart ring that was right in the center of my middle finger. "Well, for one, I'm going back to the arcade and winning you a better ring so Rose will stop annoying me about that. Hell, maybe I'll even get a matching necklace this time."

Scoffing, I shook my head. "I doubt it. Your skills haven't changed much since then. But if you play your cards right, maybe I'll win you that remote-control car."

"The red one that lights up?" He pretended to grab his

heart and sighed. But there was still a big grin spreading across his face. "Don't make any promises you can't keep."

I placed my hand over his, covering his heart. I don't know if it was just my imagination, but I swear I could feel his heart beating right through his chest. Now my smile was just as big as his. I leaned in to kiss him. Or at least tried to, but again, he pulled away at the last second. The heck? My eyes narrowed at him. "What—"

He tapped the tip of my nose with his index finger. "It's not the right time yet."

"Not the right time? What are you talking about?"

Jake glanced down at the cell phone in his hand and held up one finger. "Just wait one more minute. I promise it'll be worth it."

I still had no idea what he was talking about. Maybe he was going crazy. Or maybe I was for being in love with him. That was the only explanation I could think of for lying down beside him.

Nuzzling into his shoulder, I let out a happy sigh and closed my eyes. But it was so nice to be together again, I didn't really care what we were doing or where we were. I didn't even care that there was a stick jabbing into my thigh. Just yesterday, I didn't even know if we would ever be like this again. So I definitely wasn't going anywhere now.

"Are you ready?"

"Ready for what?"

There was a loud creak and suddenly spurts of water started drenching us from overhead. I squealed and tried to jump up, but Jake just kept a tight grip around my shoulder. "What are you doing?"

"Don't worry, it's just my sprinkler." He jabbed his thumb over his head at the sprinkler above us. "Didn't you say that kisses in the rain were the best?"

"What?"

With a twinkle in his eyes, Jake leaned over me. Droplets of water fell from his dark wet curls onto my face. "I knew that I couldn't wait until it finally rained again to kiss you, so I figured this was the next best thing. Now, do you want to prove to me that rain kisses are actually the best, or are all those shows and K-dramas basically just a bunch of crap?"

It's hard to believe, but with my dripping hair clinging to my face, bugs and grass stuck to my back, and mud seeping into my jeans, this was still the happiest moment of my life.

With a dopey grin, I cupped his face with both of my hands and pulled him down toward me. When his face was inches away, I gave him a tiny smirk. "Challenge accepted. I'm going to make you agree with me no matter what."

"I'm counting on it." His lips were still smiling when we kissed.

And I was right. Kisses in the rain were the best.

ACKNOWLEDGMENTS

IT SEEMS LIKE ONLY yesterday I was writing the acknowledgments for my first book, *The Way to Game the Walk of Shame*, yet here I am writing my second one. The amazement and joy at getting to this stage has only grown, and I hope it never goes away.

First and foremost, I'd like to thank my publisher, Jean Feiwel and the entire Swoon Reads team for being the best cheerleaders an author could ask for. Especially Carol Ly, Starr Baer, Kim Waymer, and Brittany Pearlman for their tireless effort to make *Fake It Till You Break It* as beautiful on the outside as it is on the inside.

A special thanks to Kat Brzozowski. *Fake It* would not have been written without your guidance and support. I've struggled a lot through this book and wanted to give up, but you pushed me through to the end.

To my Swoon Family. Each year our family grows more and

more, and your support just keeps on growing with it. Whether it's a shoulder to cry on, encouragement to get through edits, or an ear to rant to, you guys are always there. There's nothing more amazing than to have a squad who are going through the same journey, and I hope it never ends.

Shayda and Rachel. What can I say except thank you for always having my back. From the beginning when we were still trying to navigate the confusing and terrifying publishing waters to now. Thank you. Thank you. THANK YOU!

To my family and friends. Thanks for being in my life and shaping who I am. And especially thank you for not calling me out whenever I put your quirks and personalities in my books. Just be glad I'm not using your real names. ☺

To my sisters, the Anh sisters. I could not ask for more supportive or better sisters in my life. It was annoying being called "the last Anh" growing up, but to be honest, I was just proud to be an Anh period. Thank you for mellowing out Mom and Dad throughout the years so they basically let me do whatever I wanted in the future. Even if it meant being a penniless writer.

And thanks to Mom and Dad for being my biggest fans. I hope I'll always make you proud to be my parents, because I'm so thankful to be able to be your daughter.

Finally, my husband, Quynh. Thank you for shouldering the weight of our family so that I can pursue my dreams. Thank you for being an awesome dad to Khoi and Uyen. And thank you for supporting me even though you have no idea what I write. You may not be the most romantic guy, but you're the reason I'm able to write romances. Well, you and Korean dramas, but mainly you. I love you.

FEELING BOOKISH?

Turn the page for some

Swoonworthy EXTRAS

A COFFEE DATE

between author Jenn P. Nguyen and
her editor, Kat Brzozowski

"Getting to Know You (A Little More)"

Kat Brzozowski (KB): What book is on your nightstand now?

Jenn P. Nguyen (JN): At the moment, I'm going through my favorite romances so I'm reading *Anna and the French Kiss* by Stephanie Perkins. Fun fact, I actually met Stephanie at a convention a few years ago and totally fangirled all over her. Thankfully, she was super nice about how nerdy I was.

KB: Aw, I love that. What's your favorite word?

JN: This may seem super cheesy, but my favorite word would probably be *love*. My favorite genre is romance. It doesn't matter if it's a book, drama, TV show, or movie, as long as there's a romance plot in it—no matter how small and miniscule—I'm your girl.

KB: Do you have any strange or funny habits? Did you when you were a kid?

JN: So, when I was a kid, my dad bought me a computer typing game. It was a pyramid maze and in order to get past the monsters, you had to fight them by typing as fast as you could. Usually random words or sentences. But this program didn't teach you how to type properly, so I learned how to type with six fingers: my left index finger, left thumb, and my right hand minus the pinkie. Everyone always gives me funny looks whenever they see me write. But at least I was able to type several books this way. Plus those mummies never stood a chance!

KB: *Fake It Till You Break It* is a fake-relationship book. What's your favorite fake-relationship movie?

JN: A fake-relationship movie that I always watch whenever it's on TV is *While You Were Sleeping*. It always gives me the fluttery feels, plus you can't help but love the Callaghan family! Especially Bill Pullman. He's so swoony!

KB: This is also a favorite of mine!

"THE SWOON READS EXPERIENCE (CONTINUES!)"

KB: What's your favorite thing about being a Swoon Reads author so far?

JN: I think the best thing about being a Swoon Reads author is definitely the other Swoon authors. Even though Swoon Reads has grown tremendously, we're still a tight-knit family. We're not just names on a website. We all know each other and are able to help each other out. Whether it's brainstorming, celebrating each other's successes, or even being a shoulder to cry on during the dark times. (I'm looking at you, Editing Cave.)

KB: How has the Swoon Reads community impacted your experience as an author?

JN: There's really only one word to describe the Swoon Reads community and it's *awesome*. When you're a writer, you're often working by yourself and it can sometimes get lonely. But having the Swoon Reads community is like having a cheerleading squad behind you. Many of them have been with me since the beginning when *The Way to Game the Walk of Shame* was on the site. And their input on things like cover reveals makes me feel like they truly care.

KB: Did *The Way to Game the Walk of Shame* being published change your life? If so, how?

JN: Well, for one, I'm an actual published author now! ☺ It certainly makes going to Barnes & Noble a lot more fun. Honestly, though, it's changed my viewpoint on why I write. Before, I wrote for myself. I wrote because I *wanted* to get these stories out. But since *The Way to Game the Walk of Shame* was published, I now write with readers in mind. I write because I want to have a good story that can make other people happy.

KB: Do you have any advice for aspiring authors on the site?

JN: This may sound very boring and vague, but never give up because you never know when your big break will come.

In 2011, my older sister did her medical residency at St. Luke's Hospital in New York City, and I would visit her in Manhattan every single year. On my first trip, I remember walking in the rain to the offices of HarperCollins, standing outside the building, and thinking to myself: *One day. One day, I'll be published and walk through those doors.* My next visit, I went to Penguin and thought the same thing. The year after that was to Hachette. Finally, in 2015, my sister's final year of residency, I stopped by the beautiful Flatiron Building, where the Macmillan offices were. But this time was different. I had just parted ways with my agent and was no closer to getting published than I had been four years before. So this year, as I gazed up at the Flatiron, I decided to give up. Or at least take a break, because I was disheartened. Done.

The next morning—barely twelve hours after I left New York—I received an email from Swoon Reads asking to speak to me. And the rest was history. Ironically, I made another trip back to New York that same year, but this time I made it past the glass doors at the Flatiron to meet everyone at Swoon Reads in person. So dreams do come true, you just never know when.

KB: Where did you get the inspiration for *Fake It Till You Break It*?

JN: The inspiration for *Fake It Till You Break It* came after I had my son, Khoi Grayson. My husband's best friend had had a daughter a month before Khoi was born, and my husband kept making jokes about the two kids getting together in the future. (He said we should start setting up playdates now.) I thought it would be a fun idea to write about, so I pitched it to my editor and she gave me the thumbs-up. Funny thing, my daughter, Uyen Harper, was born a few months ago, and *my* bestie had her son a week after. Now it's our turn to set them up! Hopefully, they like each other much more than Mia and Jake do in the beginning of the novel.

KB: That's great. Second books are notoriously difficult. What was the hardest part about writing *Fake It Till You Break It*?

JN: Oh my gosh, I think the hardest part was the expectations that came with being an author. Before, I wrote with only myself in mind. But with the second novel, I had an editor and readers. It wasn't just about me anymore. And I constantly worried about whether or not this novel would be good enough. Whether I would be able to pull off another novel. For a while, I became stuck in my head and second-guessed myself a lot. This book took nearly a full year for me to write the first draft. And I gave up several times in between. Finally, I realized that I just needed to do my best and write. Luckily, everything worked out for the best.

KB: What's your process? Are you an outliner or do you just start at the beginning and make it up as you go?

JN: I love outlining! Like doodling-in-my-journal, staying-up-all-night, and staring-at-the-stars type of love. Once I have an idea in mind, I start to work on the plot: how the story will unfold with each scene, each chapter. I like to think of each chapter as an episode in a show, with a beginning, middle, and end. Then I focus on the characters themselves. How the characters will interact. How they'll feel. And how they'll look. I often spend hours looking for the right character photos for everyone. So this can go on forever. Most of the time, I get too involved in the actual outlining and it takes me ages to dive in and do the actual writing because I don't want to let go of the outline stage.

KB: What do you want readers to remember about your books?

JN: I want readers to remember to enjoy life and go for your dreams, no matter how hard or crazy it seems. No matter how old you are or difficult it seems, the only person holding you back is you.

Discussion Questions

1. Mia and Jake were childhood friends who grew apart because their moms forced them to be together. Do you think their lives would have been different if their moms had just left them alone? How?

2. If Mia and Jake's plan had worked out, do you think their families would have still remained close? Why or why not?

3. Growing up together, Mia and Jake basically knew everything about each other—good and bad. Do you think this is a positive or negative thing for a relationship? Why or why not?

4. In *Fake It Till You Break It*, there are two points of view (Jake's and Mia's). How would the book be different if there was only one point of view instead of two? Whose point of view would you choose, if it was told from only one?

5. Both Jake and Mia have passions in their lives that they end up pursuing. Could you relate to their passions? Do you have any passions of your own?

6. When do you think is the exact moment where Mia and Jake realized their feelings for each other changed? Why did their feelings change at that moment?

7. Mia decides to step in and email Finn on her own. Have you ever done the wrong thing for the right reasons? Why?

8. Which character in the novel do you think changed the most and why?

9. What was your favorite scene in the book? Why?

10. One of the author's favorite lines is "Kisses in the rain were the best." Did you have any favorite lines?

How to Pick Your Perfect K-Drama Quiz

(Courtesy of Mia Le)

1. **What do you look for in a K-drama?**
   A. Love, romance, and kisses
   B. Serious emotions and intense conflicts
   C. Unpredictable plot twists
   D. Something that keeps me on the edge of my seat
   E. I want it all

2. **What is your favorite storyline?**
   A. Cinderella story
   B. Revenge
   C. Ghosts
   D. Mysteries
   E. Epic love

3. **What would be your dream job?**
   A. Counselor
   B. Doctor
   C. Makeup artist
   D. Police officer
   E. Writer

4. **Which show would you binge-watch over one weekend?**
   A. *Jane the Virgin*
   B. *Friday Night Lights*
   C. *Stranger Things*
   D. *Supernatural*
   E. *Game of Thrones*

5. **What is your all-time favorite trope?**
   A. Secret crushes
   B. Forbidden romance
   C. Soul mate/fate
   D. Opposites attract
   E. Fake dating

If you mainly picked **A**, then you're most likely a rom-com lover and would probably enjoy *She Was Pretty*. A reverse Ugly Duckling story where long-lost childhood friends end up working at a fashion magazine together.

Notable mentions: *Reply 1997* (aka *Answer Me 1997*); *Marriage, Not Dating*; *Coffee Prince*; *Rooftop Prince*

If you mainly picked **B**, then you love your dramas and probably don't mind crying after a good movie. So *Stairway to Heaven* is definitely for you (just remember to stock up on tissues before you start)!

Notable mentions: *The Empress Ki*; *The Moon That Embraces the Sun*; *The Innocent Man*

If you mainly picked **C**, then you're definitely not afraid of the dark or things that creep at night. Try *I Hear Your Voice*, in which a high school student possesses the ability to hear what people are thinking—even the serial killer who killed his dad.

Notable mentions: *Oh My Ghost*; *Master's Sun*; *Tale of Arang*

If you mainly picked **D**, then you're definitely not satisfied just sitting and watching a drama. Get your heart pumping with *Descendants of the Sun*, an exciting love story between a soldier and a military doctor navigating the dangers of war.

Notable mentions: *City Hunter*; *Healer*; *W: Two Worlds*; *2 Weeks*

If you mainly picked **E**, then you're a person who wants everything! Romance. Action. Drama. And a little of the supernatural sprinkled in. Definitely check out Mia's pick—an all-time favorite drama—*My Love from Another Star* (aka *You Who Came from the Stars*), and you definitely won't regret it!

Notable mentions: *Kill Me, Heal Me*; *Pinocchio*; *Goblin*

Check out more books chosen for publication by readers like you.

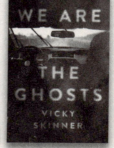